Fireside and Secrets

The Fireside Mysteries: a cozy dragon
mystery

K.E. O'Connor Books

FIRESIDE AND SECRETS

Copyright © 2023 by K.E. O'Connor

ISBN: 978-1-915378-68-2

Written by: K.E. O'Connor

Archived news articles from the decommissioned newspaper Mystical Times.

The Ithric Realm Mourns the Loss of its Majestic Dragons

By Raptor Rider

In a solemn and unprecedented announcement, the Royal Family has declared the tragic demise of the last of the realm's majestic dragons. The renowned protectors of the kingdom were reportedly plagued by an enigmatic illness that, despite the best efforts of the healers, proved insurmountable.

Lady Isolda, our revered ruler, issued a heartfelt statement, expressing the family's deep sorrow at the loss of these magnificent creatures. Dragons have been a symbol of strength, wisdom, and protection in the realm for hundreds of years, and all felt deeply their passing.

The Royal Family has implored its subjects to resist the temptation to indulge in baseless speculation regarding the circumstances of the dragons' passing. Their statement reiterated that the dragons were afflicted by a mysterious ailment that eluded all attempts at a cure. They urged their subjects to respect the privacy of the family during this time of mourning and to not spread unfounded rumors.

The dragons have long been considered not just guardians of the realm, but beloved members and supporters of the royal family. The bond between Emberthorn, Stormwing, Lady Isolda and her sons, Prince Godric and Prince Jasper, was unbreakable. Their loss is an irreplaceable void in the heart of the kingdom.

As the realm begins the mourning process, there will be an outpouring of grief and sympathy from across the kingdom. Memorial gatherings and vigils have been organized in all towns and villages, where citizens will come together to share their stories and remember the dragons' many acts of valor.

Despite their profound grief, the royal family remains committed to their duty. Lady Isolda Ithric has vowed to continue her benevolent rule, upholding the values and traditions that have long defined this prosperous realm.

While the dragons may be gone, their legacy will endure. Lady Isolda has commissioned two life-sized statues of Emberthorn and Stormwing to ensure the memory of our cherished protectors never dies.

The realm's subjects will be able to view these statues for a nominal fee and providing they bring suitable offerings of value to show their loyalty to the dragons.

A pamphlet discovered in the Ithric Castle archives.

Unveiling the Dark Secret: A Whisper from the Shadows

Author unknown

As the kingdom mourns the loss of its dragons, whispers of a chilling rumor circulate, suggesting Lady Isolda Ithric and her family played a role in the downfall of our revered protectors. This revelation is a testament to the insidious secrets that lie beneath the surface, shrouded in darkness and fear of discovery.

It is with a trembling hand that I pen these words, for the fear of retaliation looms heavily over me. Yet, the people of the realm deserve the truth, even if it casts a shadow upon the royal family who have overseen the realm for hundreds of years.

The timing of the dragons' mysterious illness raises questions that cannot be easily dismissed. It is inconceivable that these formidable creatures, who have withstood countless challenges over the centuries, could succumb to an inexplicable ailment. Could it be coincidence this misfortune befell the realm's most cherished protectors at a time when they were perceived as a threat by the family?

The secrets of the royal family, if exposed, carry dire consequences, and this whistleblower will be subjected to the wrath of those who seek to protect their grip on power.

Despite the danger, it is imperative I investigate these allegations. Subjects deserve to know if their protectors were betrayed for ulterior motives. It is a duty to honor the dragons' legacy and ensure the realm's future remains untainted by deceit.

I hope that, in bringing these rumors to light, the people of the realm will uncover the truth and decide how to move forward in the wake of this unprecedented and shocking revelation.

I implore you to tread cautiously, for in the Ithric Realm, the truth is a double-edged sword, capable of being liberating and incriminating. The path ahead is fraught with peril, but the stakes are too high to ignore the whispers that persist.

Whatever it takes, we must bring back the dragons.

Chapter 1

"Sacha should live by our rules. Heads down, noses clean, mouths shut. It's the best way to live," Hodgepodge said. "No trouble that way. And that's what's heading for the wee lassie if she doesn't show up to help with the cleaning. She's paid up until the end of the week, even though she resigned."

I briefly rested a hand against the cool side of my scaled, brown wyvern companion as he huffed and snorted his annoyance. "Sacha is never late. She could be sick. We'll have to check she's okay. Last week, she was complaining of a sore head."

"From too much maple mead! And if she is sick, we shouldn't go near her." Hodgepodge adjusted his thick tail around my neck as I dashed along the quiet stone corridor in the central atrium of the Ithric Castle. I'd learned many years ago to step lightly on the stone floor and could hurry almost silently without drawing attention. Which was absolutely the best way to live, especially when your companion wasn't strictly legal, and attracting the steely eye of any member of the royal household ended badly.

"Lady Isolda insisted on an extra clean of the dragon chamber before her son arrives," I said. "It won't be as thorough as I'd like if Sacha doesn't help. I can manage a brief tidy in between castle visitors but nothing to make the place gleam."

"It's already clean! We've been over that place with a fine-tooth comb without Sacha's help. Lazy girl. There's not even a speck of dust in the highest corner," Hodgepodge said.

"I'm not questioning orders. Whatever Lady Isolda asks for, she gets." I'd waited for ten minutes in the chilly courtyard for Sacha Dumas to show, before dashing inside the castle so I wasn't late for my shift. Something must be wrong. She was a decade younger than me, so should be through her reckless years, but Sacha still enjoyed long nights in the Pickled Badger, downing mead with the burliest of men and challenging them to arm wrestling.

"If she checks, tell her royal ladyship you cleaned the chamber with Sacha. She won't know the difference. The haughty madam hasn't done a day of cleaning in her over-privileged life," Hodgepodge said.

"I'm a terrible liar. You know that." I glanced out the window at a dull gray sky. It was late afternoon, and there was less than an hour before the royal guests arrived. The anticipation of Prince Jasper Ithric's return had spun the household into a frenzy of activity, especially since it was the first time he was presenting his betrothed to the public.

I hurried down the servants' stone staircase, along another corridor, and into the vast kitchen. Sacha had a fondness for bread, and right about now, the family leftovers would be distributed to the servants.

Alice Greenback looked up as I appeared in the kitchen door, her white hair tucked neatly under a cap. "Afternoon, Bell. Hodgepodge. If you're hungry, you'll have to wait. It's full steam ahead to prepare for the visit. Lady Isolda has ordered roast suckling, three basted geese, and five dessert options! I'm almost on my knees, and I've got two girls off with some stomach bug. I told them to go to the apothecary, but they couldn't afford his fee."

"I'm not here to fill my belly." Although the smell of sweet baked apples and cinnamon made my stomach grumble.

"I could handle food." Hodgepodge lifted his snout and inhaled. Although we weren't allowed companion animals, most of the castle servants kept their own creatures, and they were all fond of Hodgepodge, so I trusted them not to reveal my odd choice of friend.

Alice tossed him a cheese rind, which he caught in his mouth. She chuckled. "He's perfect at waste disposal."

I smiled. Hodgepodge always enjoyed his food. "I'm looking for Sacha. She's late for her afternoon shift."

Alice rubbed butter into flour with expert skill. "Haven't seen her. I assumed she was with you, cleaning the chamber for our oh-so-special guest. Five desserts! I ask you. Prince Jasper is Lady Isolda's son, not some rival noble they need to woo to top up the almost empty coffers. Rumor has it our pay will be docked again this month if they don't scrape enough money together. There'll be a mass walkout if they don't fix this mess."

"We should strike," Hodgepodge said.

"If we did, they'd easily find our replacements from the village." I glanced around, always wary of who could be listening in to report back to the family. Gossip about the royal household was forbidden, as were so many things in this unsettled realm.

Alice saw me looking and waved a flour-covered hand. "I trust everyone here. If I caught a traitor, they'd end up in next week's pie."

I grimaced, and Hodgepodge snorted smoke.

"I'm worried about Sacha," I said. "Do you think she's sick, too? Maybe this stomach bug is going around."

Alice chuckled, a deep, mirthful sound that spoke of many nights enjoying a spiced herbal pipe. "Maybe lovesick. The last time I saw her, she was starry-eyed about that new stable hand. The dark-haired one with the smoldering eyes, who always forgets to do up his shirt whenever a pretty girl is around."

"When we met him, I thought he looked cross-eyed," Hodgepodge said. "And he kept trying to look down Bell's dress."

"No doubt. He's too smug for my taste, though. Knows he's handsome, but looks aren't everything. They fade. And what are you left with? A bad character and a broken heart." Alice tossed a slice of apple for Hodgepodge, which he chewed noisily beside my ear.

"If you see Sacha, send her to the stone chamber," I said. "The prince is due soon, and Lady Isolda has been snarling at everyone to ensure things are perfect."

"I'll send her your way if she shows her face." Alice shook her head. "All this stress for one visit. And they could have given us more warning. I had to ride out at dawn to the next village to get supplies, and I won't be in bed before midnight because they always eat so late."

"It's the family's privilege," I said. "They jump, and we say how high."

"I'm too old for jumping," Alice said. "My hips even hurt when I turn too sharpish."

"So are we," Hodgepodge said. "We'll enjoy a quiet night in after the visit. Hot cocoa, feet up, snuggled under a blanket."

"Sounds idyllic," Alice said. "Save me a spot."

We left Alice chopping more fruit for the tart, and I dashed up the stairs toward my cleaning closet close to the stone chamber. I'd grab my supplies and check the chamber on my own. I had no issue with covering for Sacha. She'd do the same for me.

"Stop your fretting, lassie." Hodgepodge gently nosed my ear. "No new dust has formed in the last few hours. You've cleaned the chamber six times today."

I reached the top of the stone stairs, hurried along another corridor, and unlocked the cleaning supplies cupboard. "I always do my best in the ten minutes they give me."

The castle's dragon stone chamber was a magnificent monument to the incredible creatures that used to rule alongside the family. When the last dragon died, the family created life-sized stone statues of two of the greatest dragons who'd ever lived, Emberthorn and Stormwing. Every day, hundreds of visitors came to the castle to see them, pay tribute, and wish blessings upon the dragons for their return.

It had been twenty years since Emberthorn died, and the dragons were dearly missed by all fifty villages and towns in the Ithric Realm. It wasn't just because they'd been magnificent to look at, but because with their passing, we lost something crucial to our long-term survival.

I wheeled out my mop bucket, grabbed another bucket full of cleaning potions, brushes, and cloths, and then locked the door. I turned and almost collided with Gwit Buckleberry. I dropped my bucket, and the contents spilled across the floor.

He jumped back, narrowly avoiding being doused in my unique potion of baking powder, salt, and a dash of cleaning magic. "Sorry, Bell. My fault. I wasn't paying attention. Let me help."

"Thanks. I'm in a hurry. Big day, today." I kneeled and grabbed handfuls of cloths but then paused and inspected his pale face. "Is everything okay?"

"Yes. No. Well, I'm still looking for Maggie. It's been well over a month since I last saw her."

I dumped my cloths into the bucket and sat back on my heels. "You still haven't heard anything?" Gwit had asked for my help in finding Maggie, and I'd asked everywhere I could think of, but she'd simply vanished.

"Maggie is flighty, but she's never been gone this long." He tugged on the crumpled hem of his tunic. "I'm thinking the worst, especially with the rumors flying around."

"Rumors?" I asked.

"We're not getting involved," Hodgepodge said. "Rumors lead to problems, and we don't need problems in our lives."

"Hodgie, you love Maggie. She always feeds you raisins from her pocket whenever she sees you."

Hodgepodge huffed into my ear. "We keep our heads down, remember?"

I scratched under his chin. Hodgepodge always watched my back, and he knew if we stayed quiet and out of the way, we'd be safe. I always agreed with him, but I considered Gwit a friend. We'd started working at the castle around the same time, and he'd looked out for me and advised me to steer clear of the young princes and their wild ways. It was time to help him. Gwit was suffering, and I couldn't ignore that.

He glanced along the corridor, first left then right. "You didn't hear this from me, but I've heard gossip other women are going missing, and it has to do with the royals."

My mouth formed an 'oh' of surprise, and I blew out a breath. The Ithric family ruled strictly, and since the dragons had gone, those rules had only tightened, leaving a lingering atmosphere of fear. I understood why they were so strict. They were dealing with a crisis and had yet to find a solution, but it wasn't enjoyable living under a cloud of tension.

Gwit nodded as if I'd spoken my thoughts aloud. "I've been asking around, and more than a dozen women have gone missing."

"So many? I thought it was just Maggie. How did I not know about this?" I asked.

"Because we don't poke around in things that don't concern us," Hodgepodge grumbled. "Best thing."

Gwit placed the last of my scrubbing brushes into the bucket. "It's not just happening here. When I've been on my rounds, I've asked in other villages and towns. Two disappearances in each. Whoever is doing this, they're being careful not to get noticed by never taking too many women from one area. It's clever."

"Are you sure the women have been taken?" I asked as diplomatically as I could. Maggie was a free spirit and had once disappeared for a week, following the mystical oak tree spirit from Middle Mallow. "The women could have moved or met someone and eloped. The army passed through less than a month ago, and their uniforms always get hearts fluttering."

"And skirts lifting," Hodgepodge mumbled.

Gwit glared down a long thin nose. "My sister didn't elope nor get her head turned by a soldier. She's more sensible than that."

I held in a sigh. I knew Maggie better than Gwit realized, and a quiet life wasn't for her. She'd talked to me about adventure and going to new places, meeting new people. And she'd been a child when our last dragon died, so she had no memory of being ruled by such magnificent creatures, and she wanted to experience that. We weren't the only realm who had dragon rulers, so I understood her desire to expand her horizons. Some people were born adventurers. Some, like me and Hodgie, weren't.

"I know you've tried to find her, but will you keep looking?" Gwit asked. "When I ask around Maggie's friends, they get nervous. They see me as some fuddy duddy old fool trying to stop her fun."

I gripped the handle of the mop that stuck out of my other bucket. "I always keep an eye out for her, but not right now. We've got the royal visit soon, and I can't find Sacha. She was supposed to help me today, but she didn't show."

His face grew ashen. "Sacha is missing too?"

"Oh! No, not like Maggie. She's only been missing today. I saw Sacha yesterday."

"Are you sure? That's what happened with Maggie. One day she was here and the next gone. All of her things left behind, too."

"I didn't realize she hadn't taken her belongings," I said.

"We're not getting involved," Hodgepodge muttered. "Too risky."

"Bell, please. I wouldn't ask if I wasn't desperate. Maggie considers you a friend. She confided in you, didn't she?"

I bit my bottom lip. "Not really. I got the impression she saw me as an older, sensible sister, not really a good friend."

"Heads down, noses clean," Hodgepodge whispered in my ear. "Attention means death."

With regret, I shook my head. "Another time, Gwit. I've got so much to do, and Lady Isolda demands perfection in the chamber. Prince Jasper wants to show his bride-to-be the dragons as soon as they arrive. Apparently, she's been talking about nothing else for weeks."

I'd unintentionally eavesdropped on Lady Isolda one afternoon as she'd strode around the chamber barking orders and complaining about her son's bride-to-be for being interested in dragons, so I knew exactly what she thought of Camilla Oldsbrook. I pitied the royal bride. This family came with sharp edges and even sharper tongues.

Gwit hung his head then nodded. "I understand. I don't know what to do, though. She was my only family. I'm responsible for her. Since our parents' death, Maggie has been unsettled. I do my best, but it's never enough. Now this. She vanishes."

I released my grip on my mop and patted his shoulder. "When she returns, she'll be full of tales of adventure and most likely have a handsome young man in tow. You can scold her for leaving, but if she's found happiness elsewhere, be happy for her."

"I will. Thanks, Bell." Gwit hurried away, his hands clasped and his shoulders tense.

"Don't get us involved in anyone else's business." Hodgepodge slid down my back and hopped on the mop bucket, riding it as I dashed through the corridor to the stone chamber.

"I'm not. But he's a friend, and we like Maggie. I want to make sure nothing bad has happened to her."

"Do that, and something bad will happen to you. The family despises nosiness. Heads have rolled when they've discovered people snooping into business that doesn't concern them."

"A missing servant is our business," I said. "And if more servants go missing, it means we have to work harder. Well, I work hard while you get a free ride."

Hodgepodge curled his tail around the wooden mop handle and blew out smoke.

I turned the corner and froze. Prince Godric Ithric, Lady Isolda's youngest son, strode toward us, his head turned toward the tall guard by his side as they conversed.

My pulse fired into fear mode. I hurried to the edge of the floor-length tapestry depicting a bloody battle between the family and an ancient enemy and slid behind it, taking my cleaning equipment and Hodgepodge with me. I held my breath as their footsteps grew closer, and I closed my eyes and whispered a silent prayer to the dragons that Prince Godric wouldn't notice a human-sized lump behind the tapestry.

Hodgepodge leaned his head against my thigh, and I welcomed the comfort.

"Mother is insisting on tripling the guard on the outer walls." Prince Godric's posh, crisp tone verged on boredom. "Apparently, she thinks Jasper may be a target. I can't imagine why anyone would want that little toady dead. Unless he's bored them into insanity."

"I'll ensure it's done," the guard said. "We've had word from the advance scouts that Prince Jasper and his party have arrived at the final checkpoint and are being escorted here."

"My joy knows no bounds," Prince Godric drawled. "Let's get this over with, shall we?"

I grew lightheaded from holding my breath, but I didn't dare make a noise. It wasn't until the footsteps faded that I allowed myself to breathe.

"That was too close," I whispered to Hodgepodge. "Although I'm surprised our dour-faced posh boy is even out of bed. He usually lounges around all day, and when he gets up, drinks to excess, and then takes some poor unfortunate woman to his bed."

Hodgepodge grunted his agreement as he peeked out from underneath the tapestry.

Prince Godric's reputation was the worst, and his personality was even more twisted. I'd valued Gwit's warnings to stay away from the princes as they'd matured. I never wanted to be the unfortunate woman they summoned. Although now I'd hit my fortieth birth year, I felt certain my work-scored hands and faint wrinkles made me invisible to them. For that, I could only be grateful.

I flexed my fingers. I'd been clutching my mop handle so hard, my hand hurt. "We're safe now. Let's get to the chamber."

I'd just grabbed the handle of my mop again when something jabbed the tapestry from the other side. "Come out with your hands up."

Chapter 2

Hodgepodge hissed, his small gray tongue poking out from between his sharp teeth. I hadn't moved since the sword-like object prodded at the tapestry, looking for a target.

"I won't tell you again. Come out with your hands up if you value your life." The male voice had a deep gravelly edge to it that sounded familiar, lit with a trace of amusement.

I grabbed the edge of the tapestry, and Hodgepodge hissed again. "It's okay. He won't hurt us." I poked my head around the side. "Griffin! I thought you were a royal guard bringing up the rear to protect the prince. I almost died of fright."

Griffin Alvarez laughed as he tucked the short dagger he'd been prodding the tapestry with into a scabbard around his waist. His dark hair was neatly clipped and his firm jaw clean of scruff. "I saw you hide, and I couldn't resist teasing."

I scowled half-heartedly as I stepped out from behind the tapestry, and Hodgepodge followed. "I like my heart beating a regular, non-heart attack inducing beat. Fear isn't my friend. What are you doing inside the castle?"

Griffin grunted and adjusted his weapons belt. "Grand Dame Ravenswood saw me sweeping the yard. She paid me a pittance to run an errand for her. Apparently, I'm her special boy if I get what she needs within two hours. Even though what she needs is illegal and will get me tossed in the castle dungeon if I'm found with it."

"You'd best not get caught, then." I collected my cleaning things, but Griffin took the bucket from me without a word. It was a routine we often undertook when our paths crossed. My cleaning supplies were heavy, especially when Hodgepodge used the bucket as his own personal carriage.

"I haven't seen the Grand Dame out of her turret for months," I said as we walked toward the stone chamber. "The last I heard, she'd been locked in by Lady Isolda."

"She's escaped. And is up to mischief."

Grand Dame Ravenswood was Lady Isolda's mother. They loathed each other and spat poison every time they met.

"Lady Isolda will want her back behind lock and key so she can't disturb Prince Jasper's visit," I said.

"That must be why she broke out. She wants to meet her future granddaughter-in-law," Hodgepodge said.

Griffin nudged me. "You'll need to ensure your dragons look pretty for the visiting prince."

I laughed. "My dragons always look pretty. Although I think of them more as magnificent. The craftsmanship in the stone is immaculate. When I think I've seen every angle, something new takes my eye."

Griffin shook his head. "You're obsessed with those things."

"So is everyone. It's why the castle gets so many visitors." I glanced over my shoulder to ensure we were alone and then lowered my voice. "And if it weren't for the visitors paying a tariff to visit the dragons, the family would be in ruins."

"Hold your tongue, lassie," Hodgepodge said. "Rumors spread to the wrong ears."

"You know me, Hodgepodge," Griffin said. "I won't talk to anyone who'd cause Bell trouble. I know what happens when people say the wrong things to the wrong people." He glanced down to where his left arm should have been.

Griffin was once a member of the royal household guard. He'd led an elite unit that protected the family when they traveled. During a brutal attack, he'd lost his arm in combat, shielding Lady Isolda's carriage from marauders. Some of the cargo the family traveled with was stolen, and as a punishment, Griffin was refused magical healing. He'd been left in agony for weeks and had been close to death several times. As an additional punishment, he'd been tossed aside by the family and given a menial role in the castle, assisting in cleaning the stables and yards.

"What does the Grand Dame need you to get her?" I asked.

"A list of herbs from the prohibited list."

"What for?"

"As if I'd ask such a question. I took the coin and high-tailed it here. I figured the kitchen would have dried herbs I could pass off as the real thing. What they don't have, I can find in the kitchen herb garden. Although, if I wait long enough, Lady Isolda will catch her and drag her to the turret, so I won't need to get caught with poisonous illegal substances in my pockets."

"Stirring up trouble," Hodgepodge muttered.

"The Grand Dame loves trouble," Griffin said. "It's why they keep her locked away. She has no respect for magical laws, either. When I've been out on late summer nights, I've seen magic flashing around the turret. She tosses spells like flour in the kitchen."

"She's allowed to use whatever spell she wishes," I said. "There aren't restraints on magic use for the family."

"Only for those of us who grovel to clean their boots," Griffin said. "If you were able to use magic freely, you could clean the stone chamber in the blink of an eye."

I ducked my head. Although forbidden to use advanced magic, I occasionally flicked out a cleaning spell when time was tight or there was a cobweb in a hard-to-reach corner. It was a gray area whether that was allowed, but what harm could come from using basic cleaning spells to ensure the stone chamber was immaculate? And I always ensured there was never anyone around to see me do it.

"If you have to, you'll find the Grand Dame's herbs in no time," I said. "Weren't you a tracker before the family hired you?"

"The best. And the most highly paid, but I foolishly got my head turned by promises of riches and a house. I regret the day I ever came into the family's employ." Griffin shrugged his left shoulder. "Now, I'm useless."

"Shoveling horse dung has value," I said. "The horses love a clean bed. And the roses appreciate it."

Griffin's snort told me exactly what he thought of that. "I don't want my blade skills to get rusty. Not that anyone would ever hire me to be a swordsman."

"You're handy with all forms of blades," I said. "I value your skills in my kitchen when chopping onions. I don't know how you do it without crying."

A smile softened his sharp features. "Does that mean dinner at your place later?"

"We'll be too tired for guests." Hodgepodge was always suspicious when I had dinner with any of my male friends, but that's what we were. Just friends. "The stone chamber is staying open late in case the guests wish to visit at any time."

"Another night, then," Griffin said. "And I promise, I'll do all the chopping."

I grinned as we dashed to the entrance of the chamber. The best plans were always the simplest. Good food with friends and no stress was my idea of a perfect night.

"I'll leave you here. Enjoy your dragons." Griffin passed me the bucket of cleaning materials and hurried away.

I turned to the magnificent entrance of the stone chamber. A rich red line of carpet and a roped-off queue usually sat outside the door, but it had been removed for our guests. My stomach tensed. Even though I'd entered this room thousands of times, the sight could still take my breath away.

I wheeled my mop and bucket into the room and inhaled deeply. My eyes were drawn to the magnificent life-sized stone dragons that stood tall and majestic on display. Their intricately carved scales shimmered in the soft glow of candlelight, and the detail in their wings and claws was nothing short of astounding. The air was tinged with a faint, earthy smell, as if the very essence of the dragons lingered within the stone.

As I approached the statues, my footsteps echoed in the vast space, adding to the sense of reverence, and I could almost hear the whispers of ancient dragons, as if they were telling tales of their glorious past. It was a place of wonder and magic where the presence of these mythical creatures could be felt in every corner.

I walked around, taking my usual anticlockwise route, going from right to left around the circular room, ensuring everything was spotless. I stopped by Emberthorn and touched his giant snout. Visitors weren't supposed to touch the stone carvings, although a few did. But I always liked to touch them. I'd looked after them for such a long time, and I felt bonded to them.

Emberthorn was posed on all four feet, crouched, so his snout was level with the top of my head. His brother, Stormwing, was lifted on his back legs, his teeth bared. He'd always been the feistier of the two rulers, and his statue reflected his spicier attitude.

"It's an important day today, Emberthorn," I whispered. "This marriage is a big deal. They're already talking about a royal baby on the horizon, and the couple are yet to wed."

Hodgepodge climbed off his mop bucket ride and sat between Emberthorn's giant front feet. "He's not impressed by the idea."

"Because he knows the truth." I slid my hand over the cold stone head. "No dragons, no new babies."

Hodgepodge huffed out a breath. "Lies lead to truths if you believe them enough."

I sorted through my bucket with one hand. "Ever since the last dragon died, there hasn't been a single new birth in this realm."

"Not because of a dragon curse." Hodgepodge shook his head. "The dragons are creatures of kindness, not cruelty. They were betrayed by a family twisted by darkness. The family brought this curse on themselves."

"Hush, now. You spread rumors, but you tell me not to."

"Because I can fight back!" Hodgepodge spat out a small spark of flame and thrashed his solid tail from side to side.

"So can I!" I lifted my bleach spray bottle. "This would sting if it got into someone's eyes."

Hodgepodge chuckled. "Only if your aim is good. And I've seen you throw."

I chuckled as well. "The family has moments of goodness."

"Name one."

"They give surplus food to the poor."

"If they ruled properly, there would be no poor in need of offerings," Hodgepodge said.

"Well, they do the best they can." I traced my fingers over the intricately carved scales on Emberthorn's side. "I'd make a mess of things if I ruled. How do you look after so many people and places and ensure everything runs smoothly?"

"Like the dragons did. The realm thrived while they were co-rulers. Now they've been destroyed and look where we are."

"Hodgepodge! They weren't destroyed."

"Bell, I adore you from your little toe to the tips of your dark hair, but not even you are naïve enough to think the dragons simply died. Something killed them." Hodgepodge snuffled Emberthorn's stone foot. "And that something now controls this realm."

"What do we have here?" Prince Godric Ithric's voice echoed through the chamber, sending the hairs on the back of my neck spiking and my mouth going dry.

I turned and curtsied low, spreading my skirts out wide to conceal Hodgepodge. Prince Godric strode closer, but I kept my head down.

"I'm curious, do they talk back when you speak to them?"

I went to rise from my curtsy, but Prince Godric's hand settled on my shoulder, and he forced me to stay down.

"Well? I asked you a question. Do the dragons talk?"

"No, they never talk back," I whispered. I desperately wanted to check where Hodgepodge was. The Ithric family hated anything that vaguely resembled a dragon.

Prince Godric walked slowly around Emberthorn. He stopped by his snout and tapped it with a finger. "I don't know why people are so obsessed with them. They caused nothing but trouble when they were alive. Yet, for some unknown reason, they've been transported into sainthood. Still, I suppose it brings visitors, and money, through our doors. Mother insists they're appropriately worshipped."

I nodded, knowing the safest thing to do was to keep my mouth shut. I'd seen how Prince Godric operated when people stood up to him. The end was always bloody.

He circled Emberthorn and then Stormwing. My thighs cramped as I remained in my curtsied position with my head bowed.

"When my brother fails to deliver the fabled child, I'll convince my mother to make this place mine. Then I'll destroy these things and give this room purpose. A games room. Or it's the perfect size for feasts."

"Don't listen to him," I whispered to Emberthorn. "You'll live forever."

"What was that?" Prince Godric snapped.

"Nothing, Your Royal Highness," I said.

"Murmuring to your dragon friends again, I suppose." His laughter was cold and devoid of kindness. "We had to find someone eccentric to look after these things. They creep me out. I still remember them flying around and thumping down in the courtyard as if they owned the place. My parents being forced to speak to them and make degrading deals. What a humiliation. Far better we're in charge. Don't you agree?"

I nodded, my gaze still on the floor, my legs shaking with the effort of remaining crouched.

"Answer me. Aren't you happy to be ruled by us?"

"Of course," I whispered.

"Don't you think I'll make a magnificent ruler? With my brother out of the picture when he fails to deliver his promised child and my mother gone, it'll be time for change. Time to wipe these dragons out of everyone's memory. Starting with these ridiculous stone effigies."

I glanced up at him, unable to hold my silence. "Lady Isolda is retiring from her role?"

Prince Godric's head whipped around, and his cold gray eyes narrowed, surprise tightening his expression. He'd be handsome if cruelty didn't etch his features into a sneer mask. "Hold your tongue. My family is not your concern." He grabbed a steel-tipped scrubbing brush from my bucket and held it by my cheek. "If you want to keep that tongue, stick to what you know best. Cleaning up other people's mess and minding your business."

My gaze locked with his, and I couldn't look away. I had to. If I kept staring, he'd kill me.

"Darling, there you are." Lady Isolda Ithric swept into the room. "I need you by my side. Come with me."

Prince Godric tossed the brush to the floor and turned away from me. "I've been waiting for you. I hear my brother and his delightful bride-to-be are almost upon us. Such joy."

"I need you with me when we greet them. A united front is important." Lady Isolda was a strikingly elegant woman with a mass of dark hair set in curls. She wore a fur-trimmed purple cape and a sparkling lilac gown. She had the stature of royalty and wore a small gold crown circlet on her head. As was the custom, she ignored any servant, and we'd been trained to be deaf and blind in the family's presence. Asking Prince Godric a question had been a second of madness I regretted.

"Come, come," Lady Isolda said to her son. "I want you to change into your new robe. Only the best."

"Of course, Mother. As you desire." Prince Godric strode out as Lady Isolda talked to him, our interaction forgotten.

I groaned as I straightened my legs. "Hodgepodge! Where are you?"

"Over here. By Stormwing. There's something you need to see."

The concern in his voice had me ignoring my aching muscles as I dashed over. "I thought Prince Godric might have seen you. He came out of nowhere."

"I could hide from that half-wit in a fully lit room. That's not what has me concerned. Look at this."

I briefly patted Stormwing's claw as I hurried past. He was no less magnificent than Emberthorn, and they'd ruled side-by-side when they'd been alive. I walked past his solid left front limb and halted.

Hodgepodge sat beside a large dark smear of blood.

Chapter 3

"Are you hurt?" I dashed to join Hodgepodge, thinking he must have injured himself in his haste to hide from Prince Godric.

"It's not my blood! I found it. Or, more accurately, I smelled it."

My gaze settled on the smear. Any second, someone could come into the chamber and demand to know what we were doing. How would I explain this to them? I tore my gaze from the disturbing sight and looked around. There was no one here, but that wouldn't last for long.

I crouched beside Hodgepodge, my hand resting on his head, and stared at the blood. "How did this get here? The last time I cleaned, there were no marks on either of the dragons."

"And the place has been closed for three hours, so it didn't come from a visitor who stumbled into Stormwing and cut himself. And it must have been some injury. This blood isn't from a small wound."

The smear ran down the length of Stormwing's expansive flank. I peeked around the side again to ensure no one was watching us.

"Stop fretting," Hodgepodge said. "But clean this off before we get caught and accused of something we didn't do."

I hesitated. "Should I? What if something bad happened, and this is evidence?"

Hodgepodge huffed out a smoky breath. "Even if it is, what can you do about it?"

"I... I could make sure no one is hurt. They could be hiding."

"We're alone. There have been no visitors for hours, and the family won't be in for the private viewing until his Royal Specialness and his puffed-up bit of fluff arrive. It doesn't matter how this blood got here, but if it's here when a member of the family sees it, you'll be in trouble. It's your job to keep this place spotless. A huge smear of fresh blood is the opposite of spotless."

I ran to my cleaning bucket and returned with it. I crouched beside the stain again. "Shouldn't we report this?"

"Not to the family."

"Perhaps the guards."

Hodgepodge hissed out a breath. "Who are all loyal to the family."

"What if this is a warning?"

"About what?"

I had no answer.

"It's a warning you'll lose your head if the stone chamber isn't flawless when the visit happens. Clean it off and forget you saw it."

I mixed a small amount of soap into a dish, added cold water, and scrubbed it over the stone, holding it in place until the blood was gone. Fresh blood was easier to clean than dried.

"We'll keep this to ourselves," Hodgepodge said. "You'll only end up in trouble if you report this."

"Someone should know." I dipped my cloth into the cold water and continued rubbing the mark.

"Remember what happened to your mother when she came to the attention of the Ithric family," Hodgepodge said.

My hand lowered, and I sighed.

Hodgepodge clambered onto my lap and curled his tail around my wrist. "I didn't say that to be cruel, but you've experienced this world's unkindness and what happens when a person gets noticed by those in power. Your mother was beautiful and strong, and she spoke her mind. In a world where that's a crime, if you don't come from the right family, you know it won't end well."

"I refuse to believe power always corrupts," I said. "And her death was ruled an accident."

"By…"

"By the Ithric guards. But there was an investigation." It had been five years since my beautiful, talented mother had died in a freak accident. I missed her every day. Her laugh, her warmth, even her scatty behavior. We'd never been wealthy or influential, but the home had always been brimming with love, kindness, and encouragement.

"At least you know to keep your head down and hide. Clarice was too fiery." Hodgepodge sniffed my chin. "We live in a realm where power means trouble for those without it. We'll get past this hiccup if we keep calm heads. This blood most likely came from an accident. Or maybe it was put here as a joke, and it's not even real."

"If your nose told you it was fake blood, why did you sound so worried when you discovered it?"

He nibbled at the base of his tail, a sure sign he was anxious. "It's real. But we don't need to know how it got here. And whoever put it here is long gone."

I rested my hands on my knees. What could I do? I didn't trust the royal guard, but if word got back to the family that I'd found it and removed it, they'd ask questions I had no answers to.

Hodgepodge tensed, and the leathery ruff around his neck flared. "Someone's coming. Hide."

Panic thumped in my chest as I scuttled to the back of Stormwing and crouched under his enormous back clawed foot. Hodgepodge remained attached to me, his tail still wrapped around my wrist.

A second later, footsteps echoed around the stone chamber.

"Protect us," I whispered to Stormwing, resting a hand on one of his huge claws and closing my eyes.

The footsteps slowed then started again, slower this time and distant, suggesting they were at the far end of the chamber.

Hodgepodge hissed softly, but I shook my head and pressed a finger against my lips. We weren't doing anything wrong by being here, but if we were discovered cleaning blood off a dragon, we'd be interrogated.

The footsteps continued, and with a sinking heart, I realized they were coming closer.

"I'll attack them," Hodgepodge whispered. "I'll jump on their face and obscure their vision. You run."

"What will happen to you?" I whispered back.

"It doesn't matter. Just so long as you're safe."

"We stick together. Neither of us gets left behind, got it?" The light footsteps grew ever closer. It didn't sound like the surefooted step of a royal guard, nor the arrogant strut of a member of the family. From the way they trod, I assumed it was a female.

"Bell Blackthorn? If I'm not mistaken, this is your cleaning bucket. Where are you hiding?"

I staggered forward in relief then grabbed Hodgepodge, hoisted him onto my shoulder, and stood. "Seraphina!"

Seraphina Poldark stood beside my cleaning equipment, staring at the remaining blood on Stormwing. Her plain beige robe was tied at her waist and stopped by her ankles, her gray hair loose and flowing down her back.

Her curious expression flicked to me then the blood. "You shouldn't be here. The royal guard is about to sweep the room. Prince Jasper arrived early, and his betrothed has been twittering about seeing the stone dragons the second she stepped foot inside the castle. I've been summoned to assist with answers to her every question. You can imagine my delight at being yanked from my studies."

I took a step forward as my attention turned to the blood. "I was cleaning this off when I heard you."

"Then finish. And be quick about it." Seraphina's voice was low, with a faint gravel tone to it.

I grabbed the cloth. I had no time left to consider how the blood had gotten there. And Hodgepodge was right.

If I asked questions, I could lose much more than my job in the castle.

"Make haste," Seraphina said. "I hear the guards."

My arm ached from where I'd rubbed so fast, but the cleaning solution did its job, and there was no sign of the blood that had stained the dragon's beautiful flank. I dumped the cloth into my bucket. "I need my mop. I can't leave it behind."

Seraphina gestured for me to follow her as I turned to the main door. "No! Not that way. We'll use the stone corridors." She hurriedly guided me and Hodgepodge toward a doorway that was almost invisible to the naked eye. She slid her wrinkled hand behind a tapestry depicting Emberthorn and Stormwing, and a second later, a hole appeared in the wall. She pushed me through then swiftly followed and sealed the door shut behind us.

We walked in silence for several minutes, and I was glad of the chance to catch my breath and still my panic. There was no natural light in the corridor, but I'd used this route many times to get around the castle swiftly and avoid the family.

The passages built into the walls had been created during times of conflict when members of the royal household needed to hide from their enemies. These days, domestic staff used them, so we wouldn't bother the family as we went about our duties.

"Turn right at the end. We'll go to my room," Seraphina said softly.

"Thanks for getting me out of there," I said over my shoulder. "I panicked when I saw that blood."

"Only natural."

"I can't understand how it got there."

"Whatever the reason, it won't be good," Hodgepodge said. "It's best we don't know."

"I agree," Seraphina said.

Her tone piqued my interest. Seraphina was no slouch with dragon law. She'd spent decades working on papers and reports related to their customs. She had also written the definitive guide to the last dragon and worked as a diplomatic aid to smooth the relationship between dragons and the Ithric family when negotiations broke down.

After another ten minutes of walking, the floor angled up, and I stopped when I reached the wall.

"Allow me. I've done this route so many times, I can open it with my eyes closed." Seraphina reached around me, and her fingers pressed lightly against the wall, causing the stone to slide back.

I stepped into her warm, comfortable quarters. It was a safe, cluttered space full of books and fascinating maps of other realms. The air was always scented with the tang of ink and cedarwood. I'd spent many happy hours in here on my rare days off, plying Seraphina with questions about her time with the dragons. At first, she'd been cautious in her replies, but when she'd seen my genuine interest, she'd opened up, and her extensive knowledge enthralled me. One would think she had dragon blood running through her veins, since she had such an incredible understanding of their ways.

"We need a drink." Seraphina headed to her small kitchen, heated water, spooned herbs into two mugs, covered those herbs with apricot brandy, and then added the hot water. She placed a small bowl of lavender-flavored water on the table for Hodgepodge then brought our drinks over.

We sat in silence at her small worn wooden table, the brandy warming me and removing the fear shakes.

I set down my half-empty mug. "You didn't seem surprised about seeing blood on Stormwing."

A thin gray eyebrow lifted. "Was it blood?"

"It was," Hodgepodge said. "I smelled it as soon as we entered the chamber."

Seraphina nodded slowly. "Perhaps it was."

"Someone could have been injured," I said.

"I'm sure they were."

"Was it an accident, or did someone attack them?"

Seraphina's gaze shifted to a stack of books, and she sighed. "It was no accident."

"What do you know?" Her determined tone surprised me.

She went quiet, her hands gripped around her mug. "I fear the family grows desperate. Ever since the dragons left, things have gone badly for them."

"Some say it's a curse," I said.

"Some people should watch what they whisper. There are no secrets safe from this particularly unkind rule." Seraphina finished her drink. She topped up her mug with more than a splash of brandy this time, but I waved away her offer of a refill.

I waited for her to continue, but she just sipped and stared. "Do you know how that blood got there?"

"I fear I do." Seraphina pushed back from the table and went to her bookcase, but rather than pulling a book off the shelf, she slid her hand behind it and extracted a thin volume. She brought it back to the table and set it in front of me.

The book looked ancient, the spine cracked, and the words running down the spine so faded I couldn't read them.

"The family has been consulting me over some specific concerns, looking for answers. Although Lady Isolda is convinced her son's upcoming marriage will repair the damage when a royal infant is born, she's taking no chances. And she's not the only one who's been speaking with me."

"What question do they want answered?" I asked.

"They believe a darkness has come over the realm. They demand something be done about it. Lady Isolda is gathering information, but Prince Godric is being more proactive." Seraphina opened the book and pushed it toward me. "This is what he's most interested in."

I stared at the faded words written in a form of old English. There was a drawing of a person lying over a dead dragon. I looked up at her. "This text talks about making a sacrifice to the dragons."

"There's an ancient myth that proclaims, to bring back dragons, a sacrifice needs to be made," Seraphina said. "The sacrifice is a person. A person whose blood is supposed to be powerful enough to resurrect the dragons."

I drew in a breath. "The missing women!"

Seraphina startled, and her hand trembled as she sipped from her mug. "What do you know about that?"

I rested a finger on the image. "They've been taken as sacrifices."

"Don't get ahead of yourself, lassie," Hodgepodge said. "It's more likely they've eloped with some handsome fellow from the stables. Or gone off with the troops. All this talk of myths, cures, and sacrifices isn't real. It can't be. Our dragons are gone."

Seraphina shook her head. "Sadly, I believe it to be more serious than that."

I stared at the picture, and unease slid down my spine on an icy wave of grit. So did I.

Chapter 4

I rolled over and sighed. I'd barely slept after meeting with Seraphina and learning about the dragon sacrifice. Hodgepodge was curled beside me on my pillow. He opened one eye.

I kissed the top of his head. "I hope your dreams were sweeter than mine."

"It was hard to dream with you tossing and turning all night like you had a thistle in your knickers."

I tickled him under the chin. "Sorry, Hodgie, but you know what's on my mind. Dragon sacrifice. Is it even real?"

"If it is, unless you've developed superpowers overnight, there's nothing we can do about it."

I pulled back the curtain above my small cot and looked out at another gray morning. Dawn had yet to break, but this was my usual routine, getting up early before anyone else to look after the stone chamber and make it ready for another busy day.

"There's no point in ignoring me." Hodgepodge stretched out his limbs. "We're in no position to confront anyone about what we found in the chamber."

I set my bare feet on the wooden floorboards and lifted my arms over my head. "In a way, we have power. After all, we're invisible to most people. The family never notices the cleaning staff."

"Prince Godric noticed you yesterday. And you questioned him!"

I puffed out a breath, angry with myself for such a dumb slip. "Not smart. I wasn't paying attention. If I'd known he was going to be there, we could have both hidden."

"The best thing to do is stay hidden. We'll only bring danger to ourselves if we prod the family."

I stood and wrapped a blanket around my shoulders as I hurried to my tiny washroom. The servants in the castle were given the bare essentials, and unfortunately, that didn't include heating, so my room was often uncomfortably cold. "It'll do no harm if we keep our eyes and ears open and see what people are saying about the missing women. Maggie could be among them."

"If they're sensible, they'll keep their mouths shut." Hodgepodge balanced on the side of the washbowl as I swiftly undressed and washed myself.

"What about Gwit? Maggie has been missing for over a month. He's brokenhearted."

"He'll get over it when he finds out she's been having an adventure with a soldier." Hodgepodge grabbed my sponge in his teeth to get my attention then spat it out. "We don't want to risk what we have."

I paused from washing my face. "What do we have?"

"A home. Food. A place to sleep."

My gaze went to the single paned window. "Hodgie, I'm always afraid."

His ruff flared. "Not when you're with me."

I leaned down and kissed his head again then finished washing. "No. You're the one good thing I have."

"You have Seraphina. You're friends. And Alice is kind to us when she has time to spare."

"Seraphina tolerates my nosiness about dragons. And Alice pities me because my stomach growls every time I'm in her kitchen."

"You trust Seraphina? She trusts you. Otherwise, she wouldn't have shown you that old book. She had it hidden for a reason. It's not legal to talk about blood sacrifices."

"Okay, Seraphina is my friend."

"And Griffin likes you. I'm not sure about him, though. He has romantic designs on you."

"Griffin is a good guy. The family treated him badly, so he deserves kindness more than any of us." I grabbed my towel. "And there's nothing romantic about our friendship. He's nice but not my type."

"You make him too many dinners. You don't want him to get the wrong idea."

I grinned as I grabbed clean clothes. "What idea would that be?"

"That you have soppy feelings for him. Don't go getting swoony over someone."

"What if being swoony over Griffin makes me happy?"

Hodgepodge grunted. "I make you happy."

I laughed. "You absolutely do. And you're right, Griffin is a good friend, too. And he always makes dinner for us when he comes over. I like a man who's not a slouch in the kitchen." I hurried back to the bed and shimmied into my tailored underskirt. It was an extravagance to buy the material to make such a garment, but it was so handy. The underskirt came with numerous pockets. One was even large enough for Hodgepodge to squash into when emergencies called for such a thing, and I'd reinforced the lining so it wouldn't tear. The rest of the pockets were used for small books, treats when I could afford them, cleaning equipment, and anything else I needed.

How women managed in dresses with no pockets was beyond me. I'd saved for two months before I could afford the fabric and stayed up into the small hours for a week making it.

Hodgepodge hopped onto my shoulder and curled his tail around my neck. "This is enough for us, Bell. I don't want you ending up like one of those missing women."

"It feels wrong to ignore what we know," I said. "What we have is comfortable, and we could live like this for a long time. I make the best of any situation, but is this enough for us? Now we know what we know, can we go about our lives pretending we don't care that people are vanishing?"

"If that vanishing is connected to Prince Godric or any member of the family, we forget we ever learned about it," Hodgepodge said.

"There could be more missing people! We only know about the ones Gwit discovered on his travels, and he never goes farther than an hour from the castle. The myths about the forest witches scare him. And he didn't even know there was a problem until Maggie was taken."

"Allegedly taken," Hodgepodge said. "You'll feel like fools if you get in trouble and then Maggie shows up in a couple of weeks with a ring on her finger."

"What if she doesn't? What if we can help find her and reunite her with Gwit?"

"And get ourselves fired or worse?" Hodgepodge asked. "Once you get a black mark with this family, you're dead to any other employer. They'll ensure you never find paid work. Once you're in the Ithric family's clutches, you don't leave."

"Not unless you're in a body bag," I muttered.

"That's if they're feeling generous."

I checked my hair in the small cracked mirror and smoothed a few dark curls down, tucking them under the practical cap I wore, so my hair stayed out of the way when I worked. "We'll start with Maggie's disappearance. If we ask only about her, it won't seem so suspicious."

"It'll seem suspicious to the family if word gets back to them."

"Let's ensure word doesn't get back to them. If we hurry, we'll have time before we start work."

"Time for what?"

"Time to speak to Evander. He knows everything."

Hodgepodge hissed his displeasure. "He's a charming rogue, and he's not to be trusted."

I smiled. Evander Thorne formed alliances with anyone who could grant him a favor or get him what he needed. He'd helped me find the material for my pocketed underskirt at a discounted rate. It had cost me a month's worth of doing his darning, and that man could wear out socks, but he'd been amused by my request and said it was the first time anyone had asked for something so curiously sweet, so how could he resist?

As a result, we'd formed a friendship.

I tucked my few essentials into my pockets, locked the door, and strode into the chilly dawn morning. It was a ten-minute walk to Evander's dwelling. The servants' quarters were out of the sight line of the family, behind a stable block, but I knew all the short cuts into the center of the village.

Evander lived close to the hustle and bustle of the market square with its enticing shops and restaurants I could barely afford to poke my head inside. Calling upon him so early was risky, though. Evander worked at night, so I was uncertain what mood he'd be in.

I knocked and waited. Footsteps approached, a hatch was pulled open in the door, and Evander peered out at me. "Bell? What are you doing here?"

"I have questions. I won't be long."

His almond-shaped green eyes stared at me unblinking for several seconds, then he slid back the bolt on the door and opened it. He wore a white shirt open to the waist and dark trousers, and a belt containing various weapons and tools was cinched around his waist. His shoulder-length sandy hair looked tousled.

He ushered me inside and then closed the door. "You're lucky to find me in. I've only just gotten home."

"You've been out all night?"

Evander grinned a perfect smile. "I do my best work in the small hours. Fewer people around to notice what I'm up to." He led me into a small but elegantly fitted-out kitchen and leaned against the counter, his arms crossed over his broad chest. "Need more fabric?"

"Not yet. But maybe soon. It would be good to have a replacement underskirt. A woman can never have too many pockets."

"No doubt." His gaze ran over me, his expression curious. "What do you need?"

There was no time to waste, and Evander preferred the direct approach. "I need to know if there's truth to a rumor about women going missing from here and other villages and towns under the Ithric family rule."

A flash of surprise crossed his face before being replaced by cool indifference. "Not your business."

"Exactly what I've been saying," Hodgepodge said. "We've got enough on our plates."

Evander pointed a finger at Hodgepodge. "Listen to the lizard."

I wasn't put off so easily. "Evander! You must know about this. Your business is secrets."

He cocked his head to one side. "Is it now?"

"Yes!" His unruffled veneer wasn't fooling me. "I know what you do."

"I doubt that."

"You get things for people when they need them. Like you did with my fabric."

"I may assist people now and again for the right price. That work has nothing to do with secrets."

"That's not what I heard," Hodgepodge muttered. "But I agree with the trickster. He doesn't know anything, so let's go."

"I'll do your washing for a week," I said to Evander. "But I have to know what's going on."

Evander's eyebrows rose slowly, and he chuckled. "Make it a month, and we may have a deal."

"Two weeks. Don't push your luck. I have limited spells for laundry, and I don't want to split my skin getting stains out of your tunics."

He pursed his lips. "I'll consider it if you answer my question."

"Go on."

"Why the interest in missing people? Have you lost someone?"

"Gwit Buckleberry's sister is missing, and he thinks the family has something to do with it."

Evander gestured me to be quiet. "Be careful who you say that to. You'll be imprisoned if anyone of influence overhears you badmouthing the higher ups."

I arched a brow. "Anyone of influence is sleeping off last night's excesses."

"I'm not."

"You're a nobody, just like us," Hodgepodge said.

Evander didn't take offense at that comment. "You can get away with more if you keep out of the limelight. What have our lackluster leaders been up to?"

"When I did my final check on the stone chamber at one o'clock, it was a mess," I said. "The family must have partied around the dragons. Someone even poured wine over Emberthorn."

"Of course. The prince and his fertile fiancée are ready to do their duty, so it's natural they want to celebrate." Evander smirked, crinkling one side of his devilishly handsome face. "I wish them all the success."

"As does everyone. I'm hoping you can put my fears about Maggie to rest," I said. "I'm worried trouble has visited, and things are about to get worse."

"If trouble is here and wants to cause problems, what can you do about it?" Evander asked.

"Also my point," Hodgepodge said. "We're powerless. Even if we learn the family is up to something crooked, we can do nothing about it."

"I don't want to stir up problems, but I need to help Gwit," I said. "I'm also hopeful the rumors have no substance, and other women aren't going missing, too."

"There must be more to your nosiness than that," Evander said. "Have you seen something or overheard a conversation that's got you worried?"

I pressed my lips together. I almost trusted Evander, but he worked for people who paid him the most and, occasionally, those he pitied who couldn't afford his services, like me. "I... I found something in the stone chamber. Blood on one of the dragons. And I learned something from a book about sacrifices being made to bring back dragons."

Evander drew in a sharp breath. "Then you have seriously illegal reading material in your possession. You'd be wise to get rid of that sharpish. I know a buyer who'd be interested. He'd pay well."

"It's not mine. But now I know about the prophecy or myth or whatever it is, I can't forget. What if it's true?"

"You should forget it," Hodgepodge said. "Focus on your job. The stone dragons need you."

I petted Hodgepodge to settle him and silence his words of caution. He was always looking out for me. "Please, Evander. I have little money, so I can't pay you much, but I can make your life easier by doing your laundry. What do you say? Will you look into this mystery and see what you can find out?"

He sighed, his gaze flicking to the small window by the front door. "I'll agree to your deal. Although I should insist you do my washing for a year. You'll only use magic."

"No magic. Well, only a dash. I don't want to get in trouble with the family by using spells I shouldn't know about."

Evander chuckled and shook his head. "Why is such a good, sensible woman like you getting involved in danger? Is Gwit someone special to you?"

"Aren't all friends special?"

Evander looked away. "I wouldn't know about that."

I poked his arm with a finger. "You have friends. People who care for you. I like you."

"Bell, you like everybody! Even Lady Isolda."

My thoughts flashed to Prince Godric. "Not everybody. But most people have something good about them."

Evander pushed away from the counter. "I'll ask around and see what I can find out, but no promises. And I'd advise you to be cautious about who you talk to about this." He glanced down at his feet. "As I found out, the family is quick to ruin a person if they take against you."

I didn't know Evander's whole story, but people loved to gossip. I'd overheard a conversation about a fall from grace and Evander having to drag himself out of the gutter and start again because of something a family member did to him.

"I'd appreciate it," I said.

"You'd better. How about you cook dinner for me tonight, and I'll share what I've learned? I can bring my first load of washing, too." He flashed me a cheeky grin.

"I had a run-in with a wood nymph that left me with grass stains everywhere."

"The deal doesn't include dinner." Hodgepodge flared his leathery neck ruff and hissed at Evander.

"It's fine, Hodgie. We can have a group dinner at mine. But it'll be late, since I don't finish my shift until midnight," I said.

"A group? And there was me, thinking it would be a romantic date for two." Evander's gaze flicked to Hodgepodge. "Well, three. Third-wheeling it as usual, lizard?"

"Make a single inappropriate move toward Bell and you'll see exactly the kind of lizard I am."

I gently hushed Hodgepodge as he hissed and stamped his feet. "Group dinner it is. Griffin is invited, too. He'll do the prep. He's better with a knife than I am. Come by tonight, just after midnight."

"Bring dessert," Hodgepodge said.

Evander laughed and flicked him a lazy salute. "Looking forward to it."

Chapter 5

Griffin stood by the chopping board, a pile of deftly sliced carrots to one side, ready for the pot of lentils and mutton that was simmering. As was typical of him, he'd let himself in before I'd returned from my shift and gotten to work.

"You sure I can't do anything to help?" I almost felt guilty, curled in my shabby but comfortable chair in the corner of the room, a blanket covering my knees, Hodgepodge snuggled on my lap. I'd been half dozing, tired from a long day.

Griffin smiled and shook his head. "Stay where you are. You must be exhausted after the day you've had. I heard about last night's revelry in the stone chamber."

I didn't protest. I was bone weary and could barely keep my eyes open. When I'd gotten to the chamber after speaking to Evander, a closer inspection had revealed the family's feast had been more of a food fight, and although the food and drink had been cleared away, there had been spills and stains, and someone had crudely smeared something brown across the dragons' snouts.

There'd been so much mess, I'd barely gotten my work finished before the guards opened the doors to allow the first of the visitors in for the day. And there'd been more visitors than usual, most likely hoping to catch a glimpse of our newly arrived prince and his fiancée, so the ten minutes every hour I had to clean were a blur of activity. And with Sacha still missing, I had to do it on my own.

"Bell, how many mushrooms?" Griffin asked.

I jerked my head up. "Sorry! Use the whole bag."

"All this food, just for us?" Griffin slid the vegetables into the simmering pot.

I shifted in the chair and smoothed the blanket over my knees. I'd updated Griffin about my concerns, but I'd omitted to him that I'd asked for help to figure out this puzzle. "I know you're not a fan of Evander, but he's dropping by. I've asked him to look into the rumors about the missing women."

Griffin's nostrils flared, and he gently placed down the sharp chopping knife. "He's a slippery character, so be careful around him. Evander would sell his grandmother if he could get a high enough price for her."

"We have an understanding. We're swapping services. My laundry skills for his sleuthing ability."

"You'll be washing blood off his clothing." Griffin walked the few steps to my tiny seating area. My room was open plan, and you could see my single sleeping cot from where I sat, but I was grateful to have a roof over my head, no matter how small the space.

"Evander can be smooth, but there'd be no point in deceiving me about what's going on with these disappearances," I said.

"There would be if there was a healthy paycheck at the end of it for him."

Fast feet pounded toward my door, which burst open a second later. Astrid Nightshade stumbled inside and shut the door. Her dirty blonde hair was damp against her forehead, and she held one hand against her side.

I jumped up, but she whipped a finger to her lips and shook her head, her gray-blue eyes alight with excitement. We stood in silence as more footsteps passed the door. Astrid was tiny, barely reaching my shoulder, and although we were almost the same age, she could pass for someone ten years younger.

After a count of five, Astrid lowered her finger from her mouth and smiled, although it was more like a baring of teeth. "Hey, girl. I haven't seen you for a while, so I thought I'd stop by and catch up." She dropped her hand from her side. It was bloody.

I raced over and discovered more blood on her torn, fitted black tunic. "What have you gotten into this time?"

"Tracking some lowlife who owes another lowlife money." She glanced over my shoulder. "Hey, Griffin. Long time no see. How are the horses?"

"A lot less trouble than most people I know." Griffin scowled at her. "You shouldn't put Bell in harm's way by bringing trouble to her door."

"The trouble passed right by. Didn't you hear them? Clod-footed numpties."

"Let me see the wound," I said. "Have you been stabbed?"

"It's a flesh wound. Don't fuss." She pushed away my hands. "Hodgepodge. Looking as handsome as ever, you gorgeous baby dragon."

"And you're looking as complicated as ever." He lifted his chin so she could tickle under it.

I stared at the blood stain on Astrid's tunic. It wasn't the first time she'd shown up at my door with an injury. She'd even stayed a few nights when things had gotten rough for her. Astrid was a skilled tracker with a side order of rogue but an equally worrying side order of trouble. We'd met when she'd broken into the castle and ended up in the dragon chamber, avoiding the guards and their sharp swords. I'd hidden her in the servants' tunnels, and we'd been friendly ever since.

"Stop looking so worried. And I know what you're thinking. This is nothing like the first time we met. That time, I almost died." Astrid laughed at my startled expression. "The food smells amazing. I can't remember the last time I ate."

"It's not ready," Griffin said gruffly. "And we weren't expecting company."

Astrid chuckled then winced and gripped her side again.

I bent and inspected the wound again through the torn cloth. "This isn't so different from the first time we met. You were stabbed then as well."

"True, but I was younger and dumber. I've learned a lot since then. And I didn't have an undershirt designed to deflect a knife blow. I just need a place to hide for half an hour, and then I'll be out of your hair. Hopefully, with a bowl of that food in my stomach."

"Sit down," I said. "Griffin, get Astrid some water."

He hesitated for only a second then strode back into the kitchen, opening cupboards and removing the things he needed. Griffin had been in my kitchen so many times, he knew where things were better than I did.

Astrid waved away my offer of help as I guided her to the chair. "I can do it. You two look cozy. What's the situation? Griffin finally asked you on a date?"

"It's just dinner," I said. "Griffin's helping me with something."

"What kind of something?" She waggled her eyebrows.

"It's nothing like that. Are you sure you're okay? You've gone gray."

"I... I do feel lightheaded." Astrid's knees buckled, and she fell forward, a pained groan sliding from her lips.

I caught her and gently lowered her to the stone floor.

Griffin joined us and stared down at Astrid, holding a mug. "She always pushes herself too hard."

"She does when the Ithric family insists on something from her. I can't figure out whose side she's on. She works for them but then breaks into the castle at least once a month," I said. "Help me get her on my bed. I'll clean her wound and make sure she doesn't need stitches."

Griffin set down the mug and assisted me in carrying Astrid to my narrow bed. Her face was pale, and sweat dotted her forehead as we laid her down.

"You know why Astrid does the family's bidding, don't you?" Griffin stood back and inspected Astrid, his expression stern.

"I figured they pay her well, although I get the impression she despises them." I checked the wound and winced. It was more than a flesh wound. More complicated than I could deal with.

"With good reason. They exiled her family because of unpaid debts. Astrid works for them to repay that debt."

I drew in a breath. "I didn't know. She never said. Her whole family?"

"Both parents, her younger brother, and a sister were exiled. They were sent to Gravemore Valley."

I shuddered. Gravemore Valley was a frigid, decaying swampland. Just the name of that place made me feel cold. "That must be some debt they need to repay."

"Her father ran into trouble, lost his business and turned to gambling, which only made things worse. Then he made the biggest mistake of his life. He met Prince Godric, who offered him financial assistance. Unfortunately, that assistance came with a hefty interest rate, and when the family fell behind in the payments, he was quick to exile them." Griffin brought over a bowl of warm water and a clean cloth, which he handed to me. "I wonder if Prince Godric always had his sights set on recruiting Astrid. Her reputation is legendary."

I nodded. "He used her family to weaken her and force her hand, so she had to work for him."

Astrid could find anything you needed. There were even whispers she spied on another dragon realm, sneaking in, gathering information, and reporting to the Ithric family. It was no wonder they wanted her on their payroll if she could deceive the dragons and get away with it.

"I'll go fetch Leah," I said.

Griffin shook his head. "Stay here. I'll fetch her. I need to pick up a new batch of herbs from her, anyway."

"Your arm's troubling you?"

He grimaced as he headed to the door. "It's the phantom pains. How is it possible to feel pain in a limb you no longer have? I'll be back soon. Keep an eye on dinner. Don't let the lentils stick to the bottom of the pot or you'll be scrubbing it for an hour."

I checked Astrid was comfortable, washed her face clean of sweat and dirt, then walked into the kitchen and stirred the pot. I added herbs, salt, and pepper and stirred it again.

"You've been remarkably quiet," I said to Hodgepodge, who had curled himself into a heavy leathery necklace around my throat. "That never bodes well."

"Things are changing," he said. "We don't need these complications in our lives."

"What's so complicated? I've asked a few questions, and I'm helping a friend who's been injured." I ducked my head, knowing that wasn't the whole truth. And I knew what Hodgepodge meant. Ever since I'd learned about the missing women, I'd felt unsettled. I prided myself on keeping a low profile, getting my work done, and then closing the door on the world and remaining in my cozy cocoon with Hodgepodge. But now I was learning some stone-cold truths, I wasn't sure I could do that anymore. If I didn't, things could change, and that was always painful.

"I don't want you hurting again," Hodgepodge said. "You've been through so much, and we have a nice routine now."

"We do. It's a safe routine. A routine that has shielded us from the truth for a long time." I added more pepper as I tasted the stew. "But that's hidden us from too many truths, truths that need to be revealed."

Hodgepodge hissed softly. "Not by us!"

There was a knock on the door, but before I could open it, Evander strode in. He held up a bottle of mead and a huge tray of cherry pie. His smile faded as he saw Astrid on the bed. "What's she doing here?"

I hurried over and closed the door. "Resting. Be quiet. You don't want to wake her."

He set down the mead and pie and walked to the bed. "I doubt I'd wake her. She's unconscious. This one is always getting into scrapes. Amateur."

The door opened again, and Griffin and Leah hurried in. Leah Hawthorne had short, red spiky hair and tattoos running up the side of her face that disappeared into her hairline, depicting flowers and butterflies. She wore a long, dark cloak that covered her slim-frame, and in one hand, she had her trusty medicine bag.

She greeted everyone briefly, but her focus was fixed on Astrid. She knelt beside her and examined the wound. Leah was one of the few members of the castle staff allowed to use magic without question. The family guarded her closely, but Leah helped anyone who was sick. Her passion was caring for others, and it had caused her to butt heads with Lady Isolda more than once when she'd been discovered treating those who couldn't afford to pay. But she refused to stop, and the family needed her services, so they looked the other way, although it must grate to do so.

We hovered by the end of the bed until she glanced up at us and a thin smile crossed her lips. "You're making me nervous. Go find something useful to do."

"Is there anything I can get you to help?" I asked.

"Space. But I would appreciate more water. I need to clean the wound to see what I'm dealing with."

"Griffin, aren't you sorting dinner?" Evander asked. "You make the perfect little housewife."

Griffin ignored his jibe, brought over the bowl of water, and placed it beside Leah.

I gestured everyone away from the bed and checked on the food again.

"I'm starving." Evander strode over and stood beside me, leaning in. "Be careful of Astrid. You think I'm trouble, but she's worse."

I glanced up at him. "I wasn't turning her away. She could have died from her injury."

"I know you always want to help, but sometimes, people have gone too far to be saved." Evander grabbed bowls and set them on the counter.

I waved away his comment. Astrid was a friend, and I'd never abandon her. "Leah, will you join us for dinner?"

"No, thank you. I need to get back as soon as I've patched up Astrid. I was in the middle of mixing a tonic for Prince Jasper's fiancée."

"She's sick to the stomach of him already?" Evander lounged in the kitchen until I shooed him away.

"I ask no questions, other than those needed to confirm symptoms so I can provide the most effective remedy."

"Is she sick?" I asked.

Leah remained looking at Astrid. "It's a fertility tonic in preparation for the wedding night."

I grimaced, while Evander chuckled, and Griffin shook his head. I felt sorry for the bride-to-be. Camilla

Oldsbrook had been traded into the family as if she were nothing more than a commodity. There couldn't be a dash of affection between the couple. It was no wonder she needed something to make sure things didn't fail.

I dished up the food, set the bowls on the small table that sat between the chairs, gestured for Griffin and Evander to eat, and then walked over to Leah. "How bad is it?"

"I'm finishing the last stitch. Astrid has the luck of the dragons. An inch the other way, and she wouldn't be here. I'll finish stitching, clean the wound, and place a dressing over it. I'll leave something here for pain relief. She'll know what to do with it. She's used my services many times."

I hurried to my small dresser and pulled out a few coins, which I held out to Leah when she finished packing her bag.

She waved them away. "This wasn't your responsibility. I'll put it on Astrid's tab."

"Thanks for coming so quickly." I led her to the door.

Leah stepped out then turned back to me, her right ear lifted to the sky. "Do you hear that?"

I shook my head. "What is it?"

She rolled her shoulders. "I've been feeling unsettled for weeks. Something is in the air. Take care, Bell." Leah turned and strode into the night.

I watched her go for a second then returned and joined the others.

"Good stew," Evander said, his bowl already half empty. "I say it every time, but with these cooking skills, you'll make someone an excellent wife, Griffin."

He barked a laugh. "Was that a proposal?"

"Tempting, but I like my women a little less butch and a little more comely."

"At least I'll be useful to my wife," Griffin said. "I'm not out all hours of the night, getting up to who knows what with who knows who."

Evander laughed again. "I brought the mead and dessert. Don't all women have a sweet tooth?"

I rolled my eyes as I set down my bowl of stew, leaving some for Hodgepodge to enjoy. "Speaking of women, what have you learned about those who are missing? Is there any truth to the rumors?"

The smile faded from Evander's face. "No good news. Twelve women are missing from this village, and another thirty are gone if you expand to the three towns around us."

The food in my stomach curdled. "What's happening to them?"

Evander shrugged. "No one could answer that question. All I can suggest is you don't get involved in finding out."

"I'm not involved."

Griffin and Evander exchanged a look that made me scowl.

"I like you, Bell, but I can't protect you from the royal family if they're involved and they learn you're getting above your station," Evander said. "It's beyond even my pay grade."

My scowl deepened, and Hodgepodge lifted his nose from the bowl of stew and hissed.

Evander raised his hands. "Don't hate the messenger. You want to protect Bell, too."

I wasn't satisfied. Those women were going somewhere, and their disappearances couldn't all be linked to the troop visit or handsome stable hands turning their heads.

Evander checked the time. "I have somewhere I need to be. Enjoy my mead and dessert."

"Did your sources say anything else about the women? Were there signs of a struggle? Letters left behind? Were their things taken?" I asked.

"That'll cost you more laundry." Evander smirked at my sharp expression. "But no. No letters, and they took nothing when they left."

"Which suggests they didn't leave voluntarily," Griffin murmured.

"If you say so." Evander stood and touched my shoulder. "I know you like to help, but I don't want to see that pretty face of yours behind bars." He nodded at us and left.

I scraped the last of the stew from the bowl and fed it to Hodgepodge, not happy with Evander's response. So many women were missing, and no one was doing anything about it.

Astrid lifted her head from the bed. "If you like, I can tell you what happened to those women."

Chapter 6

I hurried over to the bed. "You're awake!"

"Well observed." Astrid's smile was in place, but it looked like an effort to keep it there. She attempted to sit but hissed out air and stopped moving.

"Go easy. I figured you'd be out for a while," I said.

"You should have stayed asleep," Hodgepodge said. "We don't need anyone else spreading more rumors and getting us into trouble."

Astrid attempted to sit again but groaned and slumped back on the pillow. "Give me a hand?"

I put my hands under her armpits and helped her shuffle upright. She grunted out several curses, and sweat bloomed on her forehead again, but she nodded her thanks.

Astrid looked over at Griffin. "Any food left? The last thing I remember, you were about to serve."

"I can get you a bowl. There's some left. How are you feeling?" He headed to the kitchen and brought over a bowl of stew, which he handed to Astrid.

"Like someone tried to gut me like a fish. Don't worry, they got far worse. It was four of them to begin with."

"Who was chasing you?" I asked.

Astrid gently lifted one shoulder. "I don't remember. And even if I did, it's best you don't know."

"Agreed. We don't need to know anything else," Hodgepodge said. "You eat your stew then leave."

Astrid smirked at him. "Are you sure you don't want to know what's going on with the missing women? Bell is interested."

I rested a hand against Hodgepodge's side. "Does it have something to do with what you were up to this evening? Is that why you were being chased?"

She spooned stew into her mouth and shook her head. We stood around the bed in silence, waiting while she ate greedily.

Astrid glanced at the small bottle left by the bed. "Leah's been here?"

"I wasn't sure how serious your injuries were. Griffin fetched her, and she stitched you up," I said.

"Another scar to add to the catalog," Astrid said. "I'll have to thank her. Griffin, make yourself useful and open the mead. I'm parched."

Griffin grumbled to himself as he walked away, but he returned a moment later, carefully balancing a tray with the mead and slices of pie on it.

"Thanks. You're an angel." Astrid grabbed a cup of mead and downed half of it.

"Who stabbed you?" Hodgepodge asked.

Astrid jutted out her bottom lip. "I thought you didn't care about me."

He flicked out his tongue. "I don't want them coming after Bell."

"They won't. They didn't see me come in." Astrid was quiet for a few seconds. "It was someone I underestimated. It won't happen again. This is all part of the job. The Ithric family wants secrets, and the people I'm extracting them from don't want to let them go."

"I'm sorry you have to do that," I said.

"Don't pity me. I can stop any time I like. I enjoy it."

I shared a look with Griffin.

"Come here, Hodgepodge. Let me see how handsome you've gotten since the last time I was here," Astrid said, her tone light as she waggled her fingers in the air.

Hodgepodge uncurled from around my neck, slid down my arm, and dropped onto the bed. He was a sucker for anyone who could give him a great belly rub. And Astrid, according to him, gave the best belly rubs. Even better than me.

Astrid finished her mead, grabbed him, rolled him over, and gave him a thorough rub. He thrashed his tail, making the odd grumbling purr he always did when he was in the throes of pleasure.

Astrid chuckled as she petted him. She held out her cup to be refilled by Griffin then looked at me. "The missing women are being taken from poor families. Families who've had their magic restricted, so they can't fight back. And those dumb enough to try are killed."

"That makes sense," Griffin said. "Whoever is taking them wouldn't want anyone coming after them. Are the women being sold?"

"Don't think so."

"The families of these missing women wouldn't all stay silent," I said. "Even if they have no power, they'd be asking friends and connections if they'd seen their missing daughters, sisters, wives."

"Perhaps they are asking, but anyone who knows anything is keeping silent because they value their life." Astrid raised her cup to her lips then paused. "Why the interest in these disappearances?"

"Gwit Buckleberry's sister is missing. Do you know her?"

"I know Gwit. Bottle maker at the castle. You two a thing?"

"We're friends. But that's not all."

"Go on," Astrid said.

"I found something in the stone chamber."

"A clue about what happened to Gwit's sister?"

I shook my head. "Blood on a dragon."

Mead spilled out of Astrid's cup and onto her hand. She licked it off with a swipe of her tongue.

My pulse quickened. "Does that mean something to you?"

"Not to me." Astrid stared at Griffin. "Did the family ever talk about the myth with you?"

Griffin paused from eating his pie. "When I worked for them, I overheard a few things. Dragon talk. Nothing concrete."

Astrid blew out a breath. "It's happening."

"Maybe. No one knows for sure."

"Hey! I feel like I'm only getting half of this conversation. What's going on?" I lifted Hodgie and placed him around my neck. He was my leathery comfort blanket.

Astrid looked away. "I never thought they'd do it. The Ithric family is insane, but they can't seriously think they can get away with doing this."

"What do you know?" Griffin asked.

"What do *you* know?" Astrid met his stare. "You used to be in their pocket, following the family around like a faithful lap dog and slamming down anyone who spoke out against them."

He glanced away. "Not for some time."

"You were still there after the dragons had gone. You helped oversee the workers in the chamber."

Griffin nodded. "During that time, there was talk of a way to bring back the dragons. I know nothing for certain, but news of blood in the chamber and women vanishing proves how desperate Lady Isolda must be becoming. If they're willing to do this..."

"Yes? Does what they're doing have to do with sacrifice?" I asked.

Astrid drew in a breath. "You already know. Oh, Bell, I wish you hadn't poked around. This is one mystery you don't want to get messed up in."

"I said this would lead to trouble," Hodgepodge muttered.

I licked my lips but pressed on. "I... I know half the information. I'm in the dark about most of it."

"That's where we should stay," Hodgepodge said. "The less we know, the better."

"I agree with Hodgepodge," Griffin said. "If this blood and sacrifice has to do with the Ithric family, they'll despise you for nosing into their business."

"I want to know where Maggie is. If we can find out where she's gone, we can get her back and home to Gwit."

"That won't be enough for you, though, will it?" Astrid said, a smirk tracing across her mouth. "I know you, Bell. I can read people. I know their thoughts and movements before they do. Now you know what's going on, you won't turn away. Rescuing one missing woman won't be enough. Not when you know there could be more involved."

"Tell me what's going on," I said evenly. "I'll make that decision for myself."

Astrid was quiet as she stared into her cup of mead. "It's best if I show you. Let's finish our pie, and then I'll take you on an adventure."

"No! No adventures." Hodgepodge coiled himself around my throat. "Adventures are for idiots. We're not idiots."

"How about another belly rub?" Astrid winked at me.

"I don't want more belly rubs. Well, I do, but I want Bell to stay out of danger more." Hodgepodge clung to me, his heartbeat fast against my neck.

"I can't tempt you toward the truth?" Astrid asked.

"There's no need to show us anything." Hodgepodge remained with me, curled protectively around my neck. "We're not involved. We've changed our minds about helping anyone. You should both leave."

"Hodgie, it feels wrong to ignore this. What's so important that you need to show it to us?" I asked Astrid.

She slid to the edge of the bed, only wincing slightly as she touched her injury. "What you need to see is inside the castle. And if I take it from its snug little hiding place, I'll be on the run for the rest of my very short life. If you want to see it, you need to come with me."

"No, no, no!" Hodgepodge stamped one of his front feet on my collarbone. "We go nowhere near danger."

"It'll give you the answers you need. Show you why the women are going missing. I thought you were interested."

"Someone else can do this. Not us," Hodgepodge said.

"I'm taking you to the original source. The reason these problems are afflicting our home," Astrid said. "Don't you want to ensure we're all safe?"

"Where do we need to go?" I asked.

"To the collection room."

I was already shaking my head and backing away. "That's for the exclusive use of the family and their guests. I'm even forbidden from cleaning in there. If I get too close to the door, a guard points a sparking stick at me and tells me to move along."

"Make sure one of those sparking sticks never touches you, or you'll be out cold for a week. That's if you survive if they have it on full power." Astrid shuddered. "Those things sting."

"Magic?" I whispered the word. It had been years since I'd witnessed such powerful attack magic. The dragons welcomed magic in the realm, but the second they were gone, laws were passed to ensure spells that maimed were restricted to an elite few.

"Of course, magic. Nasty magic. Magic you want to stay well away from. So, no dawdling if we're doing this." Astrid stood and inspected her newly stitched wound. "Nice job, Leah. I'll have to get her a thank you gift for leaving me with such a neat scar."

"Can you get us into the collection room with no one seeing?" I asked. "It's always guarded."

"It's late, and if it's the usual guards on duty, they like a drink."

"Not if it's Warwick," I said.

Astrid's top lip curled. "I'll deal with him. Do you want in or not? I was making a pit stop there anyway after dealing with the idiots who tried to kill me. I can go in alone or with you. It's no skin off my nose."

"Alone," Hodgepodge said. "We're staying here where the fire is warm and the hot cocoa is waiting for us. And Griffin can make more stew."

Griffin smiled and shook his head, a trace of concern in his eyes as he looked at Bell. "I'm done for the night."

"You're not coming with us?" I asked.

He looked down. "I'm no good to anyone. I'd only get in the way."

"You are clumsy. I've seen you trip over your own feet more than once," Astrid said.

Griffin shrugged. "Still getting used to having a lopsided balance. My risk-taking days are behind me."

"You're sure?" I pressed, not keen on going into the castle with little backup, and Griffin knew every level of the castle better than me.

"We're not going," Hodgepodge said. "Griffin is making sense."

"This is the quietest time in the castle," Astrid said. "It's the best shot we've got of sneaking in without anyone noticing."

"Can we use the servants' tunnels?" I asked.

"I always do," Astrid said.

My gaze went to the door. I was curious but also scared. "The tunnels don't lead all the way to the collection room."

"We get to the stone chamber then we enter the collection room through the only door." Astrid chuckled. "Don't look so worried. I've handled the guards plenty of times. I know exactly how to lead them away."

"I hate this," Hodgepodge whispered into my ear. "Too dangerous."

I looked at my comfortable chair with the blanket hanging over one arm then the empty bowls in the kitchen. Why did it feel like I was leaving all of this behind if I went to the castle?

"It'll take ten minutes," Astrid said. "You'll soon be back in your warm little hovel, pretending bad things don't happen, if that's what you want."

"If it helps get Maggie back, let's look," I said.

Hodgepodge hissed his disapproval, but no longer argued with me. Instead, he fell into a sullen silence as I put on my boots and fastened my cloak around my neck.

Griffin stayed behind to tidy, even though I told him to go home. But he knew where the spare key was and always locked up before leaving.

"Stay safe," he whispered as we left.

It was quiet as we strode toward the castle, veering left to avoid any guards. Guards were stationed at all the main entrances and exits, but they never monitored the servants' tunnels. Only people who worked in the castle were supposed to know about them.

We stepped into the cool, dark, low-ceilinged passage and hurried along. My racing heartbeat matched the speed of my feet as I followed Astrid. Neither of us spoke since sound traveled easily along the empty tunnels, and the last thing I wanted was any member of the family knowing we were inside at such a late hour.

"I need to leave you here," Astrid whispered as we arrived at two tunnels. "Keep going until you get to the stone chamber. I'll meet you in there."

"Where are you going?" I asked.

"To put distractions in place so no one bothers us. See you in a few minutes." Astrid turned right and headed away from us, and I took the left tunnel that led to the stone chamber.

"Astrid gives good belly rubs, but I'd give those up to get her out of our lives for good," Hodgepodge grumbled. "You'd never have done this if she didn't encourage you."

"I would if it helped Gwit and Maggie. And don't you want to know the truth?"

"I'm happy living in blissful oblivion. So should you. It's the best way to live."

I kissed him on the head. "I'm not a fan of adventuring, either. We'll do this, find out what's happening to the missing women, and pass the information on to Gwit. He can take things from there."

Hodgepodge grumbled some more as we journeyed along the chilly tunnel and came to the concealed door that led into the stone chamber. We stepped inside to a delicious silence. Every time I entered the chamber, I imagined the dragons greeting me. They were such ancient creatures with an elaborate and complicated set of protocols and behaviors, and it was easy to offend a dragon if you didn't know the right way to address them.

I briefly curtsied to Emberthorn and Stormwing.

"Don't think they'll help you if a guard catches us," Hodgepodge said.

"Even though they're gone, I think the dragons watch over us," I whispered. "Emberthorn, in particular. He was benevolent and always ready to give people second chances, even though some didn't deserve it. Isn't that right? You'd look after us if we ever got into trouble, wouldn't you?"

"Who are you talking to?" Astrid strode in through the door on the eastern side of the chamber.

My eyes widened. "What about the guards?"

She grinned. "Gone off on an important mission. They won't be back for a while." She looked around and arched an eyebrow.

My cheeks heated, but I kept my chin lifted. "I was talking to Emberthorn."

"You always talk to the statues?"

"Sure. Well, only these two. I get the impression they're listening."

"If you say so. Follow me. We have one large, particularly stubborn problem to deal with. We'll have to wait until he moves before going into the collection room."

"It's Warwick, isn't it?" I hurried after Astrid as she strode across the chamber to the door on the opposite side of the room.

"It's just our luck he's in our way. Don't worry, I've set an enticing distraction he won't be able to resist. He always prefers doing rather than standing around guarding idiots' possessions. We'll soon see him jump into action."

We reached the closed door, and Astrid opened it an inch. Warwick Woodsbane stood in the corridor outside the only way into the collection room, all terrifying two-hundred and fifty pounds of him. He wore an outfit of leather and steel, and his clean-shaven face was partially hidden in shadows, but those dark eyes missed nothing. And if he caught us spying, there'd be no getting away. Was Hodgepodge right, and this was a fool's endeavor?

I glanced over my shoulder. It wasn't too late to back out.

"Any second now," Astrid whispered, her mouth close to my ear. "Get ready for the fireworks."

I narrowed my eyes, barely holding in my cry of alarm when there was an explosion and a flash of light in the inner courtyard.

Warwick sprang into action and strode to the window, peering down. He thumped the pointed staff he held, and magic sparked on the tip, then he ran along the corridor out of sight.

"Just as I anticipated," Astrid said, her tone full of smug satisfaction as she opened the door wider and headed to the collection room. She turned when I didn't follow. "Are you giving up on me now? We're so close to victory."

"I... I'm not so sure this is a good idea."

"Your choice. You said you wanted to know about the women." She pointed at the collection room door. "The answers are in here, but the clock is ticking. Warwick won't be long."

I pressed a hand against Hodgepodge, sighed, and nodded. She was right. I had to do this. I needed to know what was making our realm unsafe.

Astrid's grin lit her face as she dashed to the door. She pressed a hand against the lock, and sparks flew out of her fingertips. The door swung open, and she stepped back so I could get a good view of what was inside.

I'd heard people talk about the family's curiosity collection room and even gotten a few glimpses when the door had been open when I'd passed by, but I wasn't expecting floor-to-ceiling glass cabinets set against every wall and numerous cabinets dotted around the room, all containing objects or books.

I stepped inside, my gaze sweeping the contents. There were jars with liquid containing odd floating objects, one of which looked like an eyeball. There were earthenware jars in glass display cabinets and piles of old books.

"You can explore another time." Astrid walked to a large glass cabinet in the center of the room. "This is what we came for." She used a spell to unlock the cabinet, opened the lid, and gestured for me to join her.

I peered in at the book. It was covered in old leather and was roughly the size of an encyclopedia. In the center of the cover was a raised image of flames and a dragon.

"Pretty, ain't it?" Astrid said. "It's a chronicle detailing the dragons' origins and, most importantly, how to destroy them."

My hands hovered over the book, my mouth dry with anticipation. "Why would anyone want to destroy them? They ensured our prosperity."

"That they did, but the Ithric family weren't so sure they needed the dragons. They thought they were better than them."

"I always knew the family were idiots." Hodgepodge was also staring at the book, his eyes wide.

"No objections from me on that description," Astrid said. "This book is crucial to understanding the dragons

and crucial to understanding how they died. And...
here's the best bit. It outlines how to bring them back."

My gaze flashed to meet hers. "We can bring them
back?"

"Oh, yes. Have you heard of the myth of the Eternal
Ember?"

Chapter 7

I shook my head, unable to look away from the book. "What does the myth say?"

"I've heard that myth," Hodgepodge said. "Don't believe a word. It's dangerous hero nonsense. Quests to save an impossible dream. Anyone who believes in it will get themselves killed."

Astrid tapped her finger on the book. "This says otherwise. Esteemed scholars who immersed themselves in dragon communities wrote it. They basically lived like dragons for years so they could learn about them. Over time, they won the dragons' trust, and the dragons shared their secrets. That was their first mistake. Once they revealed they had vulnerabilities, people exploited them."

"Why would anyone want to exploit the dragons?" I asked.

"Because not everyone has a good heart, Bell. Let me show you." Astrid carefully opened the book and turned to a page. "This section details the myth of the Eternal Ember. Basically, when you have dragons helping to rule a realm, those who live in that realm are ensured a life of stability. The dragons help to defend from threats and ensure negotiations are fair and just for all involved. They even ensure the weather is pleasant. Dragon fire is a powerful thing."

I nodded slowly. I'd lived during dragon rule, and it had been glorious. "And when the dragons are gone?"

"You get what we're currently enduring. The dragons' deaths create chaos and a descent into instability."

"The Ithric family must have known about this since they have the book in their collection," I said.

"Of course they do. And here's the kicker," Astrid said. "They thought they were stronger and better than the dragons they ruled alongside. They tried to suppress them and failed, so they came up with another plan."

Hodgepodge huffed out a breath. "More rumors. Even the most powerful magic user can't destroy a family of dragons."

Astrid pointed at the book. "They could if they knew their weakness. And they did. When the dragons refused to bend to their less favorable plans, the Ithric family killed them and placed their bones in the stone chamber. All that's left of the dragons is in that room you clean so carefully every day."

I stared at the book and then at Astrid. I was so surprised, I had no words.

"Why keep their bones?" Hodgepodge asked. "It makes little sense."

"They think they're full of magic they can exploit. The Ithric family is always looking for ways to make themselves more powerful. What's more powerful than unleashing ancient dragon magic and harnessing it for your own use?"

"They must have failed," I whispered.

Astrid nodded. "They did. Five powerful mages died trying to harness the power in the bones. They've been stored in the statues until the family can figure out how to use them without getting their heads blown off."

"If they had the right magic, they could use those bones to make themselves practically immortal," Hodgepodge murmured.

Astrid cocked her head, a wicked grin on her face. "Believe me now, do you?"

He grumbled Scottish obscenities into my ear, causing Astrid to chuckle.

"It's lucky for us they don't have that particular magic," Astrid said. "But someone does. Should the Ithric family ever find them, they'll turn them to their side or kill them for fear they'll lose control when the magic user gets their hands on the bones."

"How do you know the family killed the dragons?" I'd heard gossip about how the dragons died, but nothing had ever been confirmed.

"Because people can't keep their mouths shut when they've had too much to drink," Astrid said. "I track for the family, but that doesn't stop me from hearing things about Lady Isolda and her twisted offspring. They did it. But now everything is going wrong. They must regret the day they ended Emberthorn and Stormwing."

"They're too arrogant to care about that," Hodgepodge said.

"They should care," I said. "With the dragons dead, we have no new life."

"That's also a myth," Hodgepodge said. "Ignore this. Bell, we don't need to be involved. Let's leave before we get caught."

Hodgepodge's tail was so tight around my throat, I had to ease a finger underneath it then took a moment to calm him. "As scarily fascinating as this is, what does it have to do with Maggie going missing? The dragons' deaths can't be linked to her, can they?"

"Maggie is a pawn, as are all the women who've been taken. The Ithric family has realized their error," Astrid said. "Read this book, and you'll understand that, without the dragons, this realm will be gone in a few generations. There hasn't been a single birth since they died."

"There'll be a royal birth soon," I said. "Camilla was picked for the task. It took them months of searching before they found an ideal bride for Prince Jasper."

Astrid smirked. "The royal broodmare will fail. Sure, her family's lineage has always produced big families and healthy babies, but that won't translate when she settles here. There'll be no royal baby for this family. No baby for anyone."

I let out a sigh. "And when the baby fails to arrive, the peasants will revolt?"

"Now you're catching on," Astrid said. "The Ithric family has realized they've made a huge mistake. So, they're making a plan to bring back the dragons."

I examined a page of text and inhaled sharply. "With blood sacrifices."

"You're catching on, but there's too much to explain now, and we've got little time left. Take this." Astrid grabbed the book and thrust it toward me.

"Don't!" Hodgepodge batted away the book. "We already know too much."

"This will tell you everything you need to know," Astrid said. "The family needs the right blood to awaken the dragons, and it seems they're getting desperate enough to take dumb risks to find it."

I took the book despite Hodgepodge's protests. "You said we shouldn't remove this from the castle."

"You need to know, so you take the book. As long as we get it back before anyone notices it's gone, it won't be a problem."

"Astrid, you're a troublemaker," Hodgepodge hissed at her.

She smiled. "You'd better believe it. Now, we need to go. The fire will be out soon, and Warwick will be back, snapping and snarling if he finds us here."

I held the book close to my chest as we snuck out of the collection room. There was no sign of any guards, so we hurried back to the stone chamber. We were inside, heading to the concealed door to get into the servants' tunnels, when a familiar and unwelcome voice sounded in the corridor outside. My blood turned icy.

Astrid bared her teeth. "Prince Godric. I hate that dude. He's always skulking around at ungodly hours. Let's get out of here before he sees us."

We ran to the concealed door and slipped into the servants' tunnels, walking in silence until we were back at the exit that would lead me home.

Astrid turned to me. "Thanks for making sure I didn't die tonight. I owe you one."

I looked down at the book. "I think we're even."

"Don't be so sure about that. I'll catch up with you the next time I'm in trouble." She tickled Hodgepodge on the head then hurried away into the darkness.

I rushed home, looking over my shoulder every few seconds, convinced someone had spotted us leaving the castle and would find me with a highly important stolen book in my grasp. But we made it back unscathed, and once I'd closed the door, I leaned against it and shut my eyes, giving myself a minute to get my heartbeat back to a regular rhythm.

"Take it back or destroy it," Hodgepodge said. "Once you open that book, there'll be no going back."

I opened my eyes, pushed away from the door, and headed into the kitchen to make a soothing mug of hot cocoa. "I have to read it."

"You don't!"

"What if it's not just the missing women who are in trouble, but the dragons need our help, too? They're our friends. You heard Astrid. Their bones are in the chamber. Bones full of magic."

"Magic that no one can safely access. The dragons are big enough and ugly enough to look after themselves." Hodgepodge hopped onto the counter and stood on the book I'd placed there.

"Not when they're powerless and reduced to a pile of bones by the family they were supposed to rule alongside. They had a truce, a fair plan to rule together, and the Ithric family ripped that away." I pulled out a small tin of homemade almond cookies. I broke off a piece and fed it to Hodgepodge. "Let's see what this book has to say, and then we'll decide."

"Forget about the book and go to bed. There are only a few hours of sleep time left, and you'll be dragging yourself around the stone chamber tomorrow because you're so tired. You need to look after yourself."

"I'll sleep soon." I placed the book, the cocoa, and the cookies on a small tray, lifted Hodgepodge onto my shoulder then headed to my favorite chair. I stoked the fire back to life, curled up in my chair, a cozy blanket over my knees, and Hodgepodge settled beside me. I opened the book, fear and excitement mingling in my chest, and started to read.

Something tickled the end of my nose. I opened my eyes to discover Hodgepodge standing on my chest.

"Hurry! You're running late."

I blinked blearily and looked around. The room was chilly, the fire long burned out and only gray ash in the hearth. My protesting neck told me I'd fallen asleep in my chair and had been there for hours.

A quick check of the time had me leaping up. I had exactly ten minutes before I needed to be at work.

I had no time to change, so I splashed water on my face, smoothed down my frizzy dark hair, then pulled on my sturdy boots. "Come on, Hodgepodge. We need to run."

He leapt onto my shoulder, and I opened the door and hurried into the chilly dawn morning. "I don't know how I fell asleep after reading all of that. I expected to dream about monsters."

"Did it satiate your curiosity?" Hodgepodge asked. "You've read the dragon fantasies, and now we can go back to normal. Work, quiet time with friends, no adventures. Safety. More almond cookies. I finished what was in the tin while you slept."

"Hodgepodge, you read that book right along beside me. It was disturbing. Now we know the truth, should we ignore it?" I speed walked past shops opening and people hurrying toward the castle to start their labors, same as me.

"Anyone could have written that book. It doesn't mean it's true. Focus on what you're good at."

"Hiding and being scared?" I shook my head. "Don't we deserve more?"

"Not if it means we lose our heads."

"Is it better to lose our heads trying to do good than stay silent now we know the truth about something so terrible?" I reached the entrance and nodded at the guards as I hurried in to grab my cleaning equipment and get to work.

"What if we do something, whatever that something may be, and get caught?" Hodgepodge asked.

"I... I don't know. But it doesn't feel right to pretend we know nothing."

"We could leave. We move to another realm where no one knows us and start again."

"Why should we uproot and vanish?" I piled brushes and sponges into my bucket.

"In case someone finds out about the you-know-what you spent all night reading. Or, if you're foolish enough to pursue this, a refuge when the Ithric family comes looking for blood." Hodgepodge balanced on my shoulder, keeping a watchful eye for any family members, but it was too early for them, so it was safe for him to be visible. "What about going to that modern town we visited? Crimson Cove. We know the witch there and her talking cat, Juno. She was amusing, if full of herself. They'll help us settle in and be safe. I sensed the power simmering off both of them, so they'd help protect us."

I slowed as I checked through my cleaning bucket to ensure I had everything I needed. "I liked it there, but it's a different way of life. And thousands of miles away. And their way of doing things is odd. Too fast-paced."

"They use magic freely, and there's no fear of being murdered."

"You say that, but Zandra and Juno were investigating a murder when we first met them. It's not as safe as it seems."

"They have angels to protect them."

"Those angels weren't doing a great job, though, were they? Juno had to assist them in solving a crime." I shook my head as I headed to the stone chamber. "Running away won't fix the problem. It'll pass it on to somebody else."

"Then let it pass to them! They can die, and we'll live to clean for another day and then relax with hot cocoa and almond cookies."

I could already see the guards who looked after the stone chamber approaching the entrance, so I hurried inside, checked no one was in there, and then threw out a basic cleaning spell that whirled around the room in a mini-tornado, collecting dust or debris I'd missed the previous evening. I only ever used the spell in emergency situations, and it was a gray area whether I should use it. The family didn't like anyone using magic, but sometimes, it was a necessity.

"You could use that spell all the time if we lived somewhere else," Hodgepodge said.

I flexed my fingers. It felt incredible to use magic. We all had it, some of us more than others, and there was nothing more natural than having a spell you were born to do slide out and weave around you. I got restless if I didn't use my magic, and the less I used, the less confident I became in casting spells. Perhaps that was what the family wanted. If people didn't use magic, they were weaker and easier to control.

I tapped my knuckles against the side of my head. Too much thinking was never a good thing.

"I'll tell Astrid we don't want the book," Hodgepodge said, as we inspected the chamber to ensure nothing had been missed and everything was perfect for the first visitors of the day.

I stopped by Emberthorn and rested my head on his snout. "We have a dilemma, old friend. Maybe you can help." The remains of my spell whirled around me and lifted my hair. For a second, it felt like Emberthorn was talking back to me, or at least, giving me a sign he was paying attention.

A guard poked his head inside the chamber. "Everything good to go, Bell? We're opening the doors in three minutes."

I lifted my head and raised a hand at the same time. "All good. The dragons are looking forward to welcoming their visitors."

He shook his head and rolled his eyes. "Sure thing, dragon lady."

I was used to being mocked for spending so much time with the stone dragons, but I felt connected to them. Even though real dragons were gone from this realm, I still expected to see one as I walked around a corner.

And now I knew their bones were hidden inside the statues, there was even more of a connection to them.

"Emberthorn's not going to answer you," Hodgepodge said. "He never does."

"Maybe not. But talking through this problem helps. What if those missing women are being mistreated? Who knows how much of their blood is being drained and smeared on the dragons?"

"Hardly any. That was the first smear of blood we've ever seen in here."

I stepped back from Emberthorn. "Or it was the first smear of blood whoever is doing this missed. They're careful to clean up after themselves, so they can hide what they're doing. We can't let this happen."

"How are we supposed to stop it? We have no power or influence."

I rested a hand back on Emberthorn's snout. "I have no clue. We need to read more of that book. There could be answers in there."

"We've read enough. Any more will lead us along the path we don't want to tread."

"Maybe we don't want to do it, but we should."

Hodgepodge snorted his displeasure. "Leave it to Astrid. She's the tracker. She loves an adventure. Or Evander. He's dumb enough to chase a quest that'll lead to certain doom."

"I don't think anyone has enough money to pay Evander to take on something so risky." I grabbed my cleaning bucket and hurried out of the room, nodding at the guards. The first crowd of visitors for the day was already approaching. I was cutting it fine.

My stomach growled at the same time as Hodgepodge's. "Let's go to the kitchen. See if there are any leftovers."

"That's the first sensible thing you've said this morning." Hodgepodge tucked his tail around my neck and settled in for the ride.

I had fifty minutes until the chamber closed and I needed to clean again, so I put away my supplies and strolled along the stone corridor. The castle was starkly beautiful with impressive tapestries on some walls, but it always had a cold, oppressive feeling, as if someone had whisked through it and sucked away the joy. Even the rooms with blazing hearths never felt welcoming.

"If I owned this place, I'd have color everywhere," I said. "More light, flowing fabrics, cozy chairs, and corners where people could curl up and rest or read or simply look out of the window and observe the comings and goings in the courtyard. Make it a much more welcoming place."

"The Ithric family doesn't want to welcome people. They want to intimidate them and scare them into subservience," Hodgepodge said.

I looked around, but we were alone, so we could indulge our fantasies. "You'd have your very own room. Maybe an entire turret."

He chuffed out a laugh. "I'd like that. I like being up high. I could look out across the realm from the top of the turret. I could sit on the roof and inspect my kingdom."

"Our kingdom. We'd rule jointly, just as the family did with the dragons."

I entered the kitchen to find two small groups gathered together, whispering with each other.

Alice Greenback raised her head when she saw me. "Come to get the newest gossip, I suppose?"

"No, I didn't have time for breakfast this morning. Have you got any leftovers?"

"It's not like you to be disorganized. Over there. There's a pot of barley simmering, and there's cream and sugar. There are vegetable peelings in the usual place for Hodgepodge."

"Thanks." I grabbed a bowl and spoon and sorted breakfast for us both, picking out plump grapes and wilted spinach for Hodgepodge. "What's the latest gossip?"

Alice raised an eyebrow as she deftly kneaded bread and ignored the whispering groups. "Someone was crazy enough to break into the castle last night and steal from the family."

I almost choked on my barley. "Do they know who did it?"

"Not yet. But everyone is under suspicion."

"What was taken?" My spoon clattered against the bowl as my hand shook.

"Nobody knows, but it was something important." Alice leaned closer. "Watch out. They're planning on interrogating everyone until they find out who did it."

Chapter 8

"They won't want to speak to us. We're nobodies." Hodgepodge was tucked into the largest pocket of my underskirt as I swept the public walkway through the stone chamber.

"According to Alice, everyone is being interrogated." My hands slipped on the broom, and it clattered to the floor. I wiped my damp palms down my skirt. It wasn't yet midday, and the chamber had received a steady flow of visitors since the doors opened, so I'd been kept on my toes, but I was struggling to concentrate. The Ithric family knew about the break-in, and they wanted revenge.

"We're safe. They never notice us." Hodgepodge's voice was muffled in my skirt. Even though he tried to reassure me with his words, his actions revealed his nerves. He only ever hid in my underskirt pocket when he was anxious or had to duck out of sight and had no other option.

I rested against Stormwing for a moment to catch my breath. I turned my head as someone whispered my name. My gaze darted around, but the chamber was empty. "Hello? Is someone in here? The chamber doesn't open for another few minutes."

My murmured name sounded again. I pushed away from Stormwing and walked around him and then turned on my heel.

"Is something wrong?" Hodgepodge asked.

"Didn't you hear that voice?"

"It's just us in here. But it won't be soon. We need to get out before they open the doors again and the rowdy worshippers descend on the dragons."

I did another quick check to convince myself we were alone, grabbed my cleaning things, and hurried out. The tiredness and stress must be getting to me.

"We need to find another servant the guards have already interviewed, so we know what questions they'll ask me when it's my turn," I muttered as I checked the time.

"Go back to the kitchen. Someone in there must have been interviewed by now," Hodgepodge said.

I swiftly tucked away my cleaning equipment, took a few calming breaths, then hurried toward the kitchen. Servants were bustling in and out with trays of food for the family's extravagant lunch.

I ducked my head into the kitchen to find Alice laying out platters of sliced meats and instructing servers.

"Back for more food?" she asked when she spotted me.

"No, I'm good, thanks. Have they interviewed you yet about the stolen items?"

Alice grunted. "They know better than to drag me away from the kitchen when the family is making demands for food. No one can run this kitchen like I can."

My heart sank. "No one in here has been questioned?"

"Not without my permission. The family may own this castle, but if they want delicious meals, they won't interfere. They're dining out tonight, so I expect we'll get quizzed this afternoon. How about you?" Alice deftly assembled a tray of delicacies.

"No. They won't want to talk to the cleaners, surely. I keep my head down and see nothing."

"As I understand it, no one's escaping the questioning. Although, I suppose if they find out who broke in before they get to you, they won't bother to haul you over the coals." She glanced up at me, and her gaze narrowed. "Do you know something?"

"No! I just want to get it over with. It makes me nervous waiting to be summoned for something I know nothing about."

"If that's so, you won't mind coming with me now." Warwick Woodsbane loomed in the kitchen doorway, his pointed staff strapped to his back and a sparking stick in his hand.

I took a step back. "I'm... I'm on cleaning duty at the stone chamber."

"And you've just finished, so you're not needed for almost an hour. Follow me." His stern tone left no room for debate, not that I'd dare debate with someone who could crush me with a stern look.

"You'll be fine." Alice's smile held a hint of worry. "You don't know anything, so you can't get in trouble. Keep your answers short and to the point and get out as quickly as you can. Do you want to leave Hodgepodge here?"

"I'm going with Bell." His voice drifted out of my pocket.

I should leave Hodgepodge in the warmth and safety of the kitchen, where he'd be fed treats and get tickles, but I needed support if I was going into the demon's den.

"Here, catch this. You can reward yourself when it's over." Alice threw me a handmade boiled candy, which I thanked her for and tucked into a pocket. I dashed after Warwick to find him already halfway along the corridor.

He didn't look back as he led me to a room, the door standing open. I'd never been inside this room, but it was arranged as a study with an expensive looking wooden desk, chairs, and tall bookshelves lining the walls. The scent of lemon polish and pipe smoke drifted in the chilly air.

"Take a seat," Warwick said.

I did as ordered and settled on the edge of a wooden chair, my back straight, my hands clenched in my lap. I slid a finger between the slit in my skirt, and Hodgepodge grabbed it with his tail.

Warwick strode around the room, looking out of each window in turn.

"Should I start?" I asked.

"We're waiting for someone to join us."

"You're not questioning me?"

"Unfortunately, not," he murmured.

I shifted in my seat, attempting to look more relaxed despite my racing heartbeat. I'd follow Alice's advice. Keep my answers short, don't stray from the point, and get out as soon as I can. I touched the boiled candy in my pocket. That would be my reward when I got out the other side.

I adjusted my skirt so Hodgepodge lay more comfortably on my lap without it appearing obvious I had a chunky wyvern hidden beneath the folds. When he wanted to, he could curl into a tight ball and appear half the size he was, but he was still heavy.

Footsteps approached the room, and I turned. My hope of getting out easily died as Prince Godric appeared. He held a plate of crackers and cheese in one hand and a goblet of what must be wine in the other. No matter the hour, the prince adored his wine. Vast amounts were imported from across the world in his desire to find the perfect sozzle sauce.

"This is Bell Blackthorn." Warwick approached the table and waited until Prince Godric sat before joining him.

I looked at Warwick in surprise, amazed he knew my name, but then he was a member of the Royal Guard. It was his business to know everything that went on in the castle and who was doing it.

"What do you do for us, Bell?" Prince Godric asked, not looking at me as he inspected the cheese.

"I clean, Your Royal Highness. Mainly the stone chamber. I look after the dragons and make sure everything is as it should be for our visitors."

"Our visitors?" Prince Godric arched an eyebrow, still sorting over his food. "Are you a member of the household? Do I have a sister I know nothing about? In his heyday, my father was known to stray, so it's entirely possible. Although you didn't hear that from me."

I gulped. "I meant your visitors. Of course, this castle belongs to you, sir."

He chuckled, snapped a cracker in half, and popped it into his mouth. "Not yet. Soon. I assume you've heard the rumors."

"I... I believe something's been taken."

Prince Godric's eyes narrowed as they finally flicked my way. "Servants shouldn't gossip, especially not about my family. Idle tongues disappear from mouths. Isn't that right, Warwick?"

Warwick bowed his head. "It has been known."

"Sorry. I didn't mean to gossip."

Prince Godric waved a hand in the air. "So, what do you know?"

I swallowed my nerves. "Very little."

"What are your hours in the castle?"

"I start at five in the morning and stay until midnight. The last tour of the stone chamber takes place at eleven, and then I conduct a final inspection before the chamber shuts for the night."

"Which means you were here late last night. Did you see anyone prowling around looking suspicious?"

"No! I saw no one suspicious. I was tired after a long day of work and ready to return home."

"Tired? You clean for ten minutes an hour. That's hardly exhausting. I'm surprised we even pay you. It's a privileged to work for us, don't you think?"

I glanced at Warwick, but his dark gaze had settled an inch above my head, giving away nothing. "That's true. Sometimes your visitors are messy, though, and the stone chamber is huge."

"The peasants have nothing to do with me," Prince Godric said. "If I had a choice, I'd ban them."

"No. They don't. I didn't mean that. I meant…" My words left me, and I could only stare at Prince Godric. His chin was stubbled, his hair greasy, and he had a wine stain on his expensive embroidered tunic. His mother must have dragged him out of bed to conduct these interviews.

Hodgepodge squeezed my finger so hard, I almost squeaked.

Prince Godric smirked. "Go on. You finished your day of drudgery, and then what happened?"

"I had friends over for a late supper. We ate stew."

"Handy. You concocted yourself an alibi."

I jerked in my seat. "I didn't! We'd already arranged the dinner before the theft took place."

Prince Godric sipped his wine and leaned back in his chair. "Warwick, get the names then check if she's lying to me."

Warwick nodded and made a note on the paper in front of him as I told him who I had supper with. I left off Astrid and Evander. If Prince Godric knew I was friendly with them, it would raise his suspicions about me.

Prince Godric yawned. "I'm bored with this. Fill in the gaps so she can gossip with her friends when this is over," he said to Warwick.

"Of course, sir. Three significant items were taken from the castle last night between the hours of midnight and two o'clock in the morning," Warwick said, his tone flat, suggesting he'd repeated these words a dozen times or more already.

"What were they?" I asked.

"An ancient sacred text from the collection room," Warwick said, "a bag of gold coins, and a recently purchased engagement ring from Prince Jasper's private quarters."

"That ring should have been on the silly creature's finger. It's Camilla's fault she lost her diamonds. Why remove it?" Prince Godric mused. "Is it a sign the impending marriage is already in trouble?"

Hodgepodge shifted on my lap, and I could imagine what he was thinking. Astrid had brought us into the castle under the pretense of obtaining the book, and in the meantime, she'd stolen from the family she was supposed to work for. She hadn't been helping me. She'd had her own mission to complete.

"What would you do if you came into ownership of expensive coins, a valuable ring, and a boring old book that some people lose their minds over?" Prince Godric asked, still more interested in his food than me.

"If they weren't mine, I'd return them," I said. "Of course, I'd need to know who they belonged to before I could do that."

"So you could ransom them?"

My eyes widened, but I kept my composure. "I wouldn't know how to ransom anything. I live a simple life. I want no trouble."

"Bell returns the coins visitors drop," Warwick said.

I stared at him. I had no clue he'd seen me do that. "Many visitors have little to spare."

Warwick simply nodded in reply.

"I can't imagine many other servants would give back something another was too foolish to keep hold of," Prince Godric said. "Finders keepers in my eyes."

"That's one way of looking at it," I mumbled.

"Such a good little cleaner," Prince Godric said. "How did we ever manage without you?"

I lowered my head. I needed to stop talking, but my nerves were getting the better of me.

"Look at me," Prince Godric said.

I raised my head and met his gaze.

"Oh! It's you. You're the weird one who talks to the stone dragons. I remember you."

"I... I talk to myself when I'm cleaning them."

"I overheard you the other day. Why? It's not as if they can talk back." His gaze lit with a cold interest that made my stomach churn. "Can they? Have they done anything to alarm you?"

His coolly elusive questions didn't fool me. If Prince Godric was the family member stealing women and using them to bring back the dragons, he'd know about the blood sacrifices. He must have read the stolen book, which was currently hiding underneath the mattress in my room.

"Answer the prince," Warwick said sharply.

I jumped in my seat. "The dragons don't talk to me. Stone can't talk."

"Why do you talk to them, then?" Prince Godric tapped a finger on the table. "I know you do. I've heard my guards' comments about the strange cleaner who spends more time with statues than people. You have an affinity with them?"

"I don't. But you're right, I spend my working time with the dragons, and it's usually just me or one other cleaner. Recently, I've been on my own since Sacha disappeared."

"Disappeared? What's this? We have serving girls going missing, Warwick?" Godric lounged back in his seat and munched on some crackers.

"Not that I'm aware of, sir."

"Not disappeared," I hastened to add. "She may have moved away or gotten another job. Sacha's yet to be replaced, so I'm on my own. Sometimes, I need to get something off my chest, so..."

"You talk to the dragons." Prince Godric chuckled to himself. "How odd. I sometimes wonder who we employ in this place. Lunatics, halfwits, and beggars, by the sounds of it."

"Bell is thorough in her chamber duties," Warwick said. "The guards think highly of her, despite her eccentric behavior."

"With eyes as lovely as that, I'm sure they do." Prince Godric smirked. "If you were a few years younger... still, there's always room to experiment."

I bit my tongue. The more I said, the worse this became. I didn't have an alibi, but Astrid wouldn't say a word about me being in the castle since she'd stolen most of the items, and I could rely on Griffin to be quiet. As for Evander, I was undecided, but I almost trusted him.

"Has anyone spoken to you about the stolen items?" Prince Godric asked.

"No! Everyone's busy working as usual."

"If you hear anything, tell Warwick. When these items are retrieved, there'll be a reward for the person who provides the most valuable information." Prince Godric drained his goblet. "And let it be known that, when the thief is discovered, they'll receive the harshest punishment. Stealing from my family is unforgivable."

I nodded swiftly. "Most people don't listen to me, but I'll tell anyone who asks."

Prince Godric hummed under his breath, his expression sardonic. "I suppose the only individuals who listen to you are those stone caricatures you fuss around so much."

I bowed my head. Better to look kooky and quiet and hope he'd forget me again.

"Warwick, get any details you need then bring in the next servant. And find me more wine. This muck has been watered down."

"Very good." Warwick stood and gestured for me to follow him to the door. "You can leave."

"Be seeing you, little cleaner," Prince Godric called out.

I curtsied before dashing away.

Warwick squeezed my elbow before I could flee too far. "Remember what Prince Godric said. Any information, you come to me first. Not him."

I nodded.

"This isn't a joke. Don't go to Prince Godric. Not for anything."

My gaze flicked over Warwick. Was that a warning not to bother the prince or a warning it wasn't safe to be alone with him?

I opened my mouth to ask, but he let go of my elbow and shooed me away. That was all the warning I needed.

I turned the corner and leaned against the wall before my knees gave out. What had I gotten myself into?

Chapter 9

The swell of visitors hadn't abated, and by mid-afternoon, my stomach was growling. I finally got away from the castle in need of fresh air. Hodgepodge snuggled himself around my neck as I reached the market to browse the food stalls and pick something cheap and tasty to eat.

"I'm in the mood for pie," Hodgepodge said.

"Sweet or savory?" I paused and inspected a food stall, even though all the treats were out of my price range. I didn't usually buy lunch, making do with leftovers from the previous evening's dinner, but there hadn't been a scrap of stew left from last night, and with the distractions caused by everything else going on, I'd been less than prepared this morning.

"Sweet pie. I don't like Evander, but he brings amazing desserts to our suppers. I've been thinking about that pie he delivered all day."

"Let's hope he brings us an amazing alibi if Warwick and Prince Godric learn we had supper together," I murmured.

"Bell! I thought that was you." Gwit strode over. "Late lunch?"

I nodded. "It's been so busy at the castle since Prince Jasper and his betrothed arrived, I've barely had a chance to catch my breath. I think the visitors are hoping to catch a glimpse of them. They've been queuing for ages to get into the stone chamber and nose around."

"No doubt, leaving a mess for you to clear." Gwit shook his head. "Mind if I join you? I've been working all morning and haven't had a chance for a break, either."

"Of course. We were just figuring out what to eat."

"Maggie loved spiced damson pie. There's a seller at the end of the row who makes them fresh each day. Tart and sweet. She once ate an entire pie in one sitting and had purple stains on her fingers for days."

I smiled as he recalled the memory while we walked past more market stalls, the hustle and bustle of village life all around us and the calls of market traders ringing in the crisp air. "Any news from Maggie?"

Gwit shook his head, and his smile faded. "It feels as if she's vanished. As if someone picked her up and took her somewhere far away where she can't contact me."

"Did Maggie ever use the portal tunnels?" Hodgepodge asked. "They can take you hundreds of miles in a few heartbeats if you use the right magic."

"Occasionally, but we had little reason to travel far," Gwit said. "And where would she go? Our whole world is here."

"Perhaps she decided to have an adventure." I didn't want to get Gwit's expectations up, since I thought it likely Maggie had been taken by the Ithric family, but until I had proof, I was reluctant to crush his hopes of her safe return.

"My sister was a dreamer rather than a doer. She liked the occasional adventure, but she preferred her home comforts. And although she could be willful, she was never cruelly disobedient. Maggie wouldn't up and leave without telling me because she knows I'd be heartbroken to lose her. If she was going on a long adventure, she'd ask me to go with her. And, the fool I am, I most likely would. Anything to keep my sister happy and safe."

"And leave all of this?" I gestured around the bustling market, stepping aside to avoid being trodden on by a goods ladened mule with a red and yellow frilled neck tie.

He smiled. "Life here isn't so bad. Of course, it was better when we had dragons looking after us. But we do the best we can, and that's all we can ask of ourselves and others."

We stopped by the pie stall. The queue of people waiting to be served suggested the food was excellent and worth the wait.

"Did you hear about the thefts at the castle?" I asked.

Gwit glanced around. "I did. Everyone working in the bottle factory has been questioned. I'm amazed. I can't remember the last time anything was stolen from the castle. The family will come down hard on the guards for this mistake."

"I hadn't thought about that," I said.

Gwit nodded. "I heard someone started a fire in the courtyard. It distracted the guards from their stations. And, you didn't hear this from me, Warwick was scolded because he left his post outside the collection room. Because he wasn't there, someone snuck in and stole a book. Something to do with dragons if you believe the gossip."

"You know about the missing book?"

"I've never seen it, but I've worked here long enough to know the collection room is full of incredible curiosities, many containing powerful magic or information that can make an individual extremely dangerous. The family is livid. They see it as an embarrassment because they were unable to protect their home."

"It's not the guards' fault someone broke in." We inched forward in the queue. "They needed to ensure the fire didn't spread. They wouldn't have wanted the stables burned or the horses injured."

"Of course. But whoever snuck into the castle made a mockery of their protection."

"I heard other things were taken, too." I feigned an air of not being bothered while hiding my intense desire to learn everything I could.

"They were. Gold and jewels. Nothing so strange about that, but it makes me wonder if whoever entered the castle was targeting that book. There must be something important in it."

I was quiet for a few seconds. "I guess there must."

"Have they spoken to you?"

"Warwick and Prince Godric questioned me."

Gwit turned and stared at me. "Prince Godric was in your interview?"

"Yes. Wasn't he in yours?"

"No, just two guards. Why is he interested in you?"

A coil of dread swirled around my stomach, and it felt like a fist squeezed my heart. "He's not! He must have dropped by to see how things were going. He was more interested in his cheese and crackers than speaking to me."

Gwit's pale forehead furrowed. "Be careful of Prince Godric. He's a bad guy who has too much power, and he thinks he's untouchable."

"Given the amount of power the family has, he kind of is," I muttered.

We were almost at the front of the queue, and I took a few seconds to distract myself by reading through the delicious descriptions of the pies. Every corner I turned drew me closer to Prince Godric being the ringleader for stealing women and using them to get back what, if the gossip was true, his family had destroyed.

"I'm having damson. It's what Maggie would order if she were here." Gwit's eyes glazed with tears, and he looked away.

"Damson sounds perfect. I'll have that, too." I gave Gwit a moment to compose himself while I checked through my pockets for a few coins. "Do you remember what Maggie was doing on the day she vanished?"

Gwit nodded then placed the order, waving away my money. "This is my treat. It's good to talk about my sister. You're the only one who listens. Now she's gone, everyone's forgotten about her."

"You never will. And she'll come back. Don't give up hope."

"I won't. I'll keep looking until I know the truth." He took the two plates of pie the server held out, and we walked away and found a small bench to sit on.

I sampled the damson pie. It was as delicious as Gwit had described, the pastry buttery and crumbly and the filling sweet with a zing of sour. I broke off a small piece and fed it to Hodgepodge. "So, your sister? What was she doing just before she went missing?"

"Maggie was excited because she had a new job. She'd been hired to transport documents to a neighboring town for the family."

"That's a step up!" I said.

"The opportunity came out of the blue. It was good money, and she jumped at the chance to do something different. Maggie said it would get her out of this backward little dive – her words - and she'd get to see more of the world."

"How long had she been doing that before she vanished?"

Gwit considered the question as he ate his pie. "A few weeks. Maggie made three trips over the space of a week. Each time, she'd collect the documents that needed to be taken and then head off."

"How long was she gone?"

"They were mainly day trips. There was one occasion when she stayed overnight, but she was back early the next day. She said she didn't want me to worry and think an ogre had stolen her away." Gwit's laughter was sadness-tinged.

"Did Maggie ever say anything about being followed or watched or give you concerns for her safety?" I asked.

"Nothing like that. But she disappeared on her last job. She collected the paperwork as usual, said she'd be gone all day, and set off. When she didn't show up late that evening, I assumed she'd been delayed or there was a problem on the road, so she'd stayed somewhere overnight. I wasn't concerned. But when Maggie didn't show the next day, I got worried."

"How long was she gone before you looked for her?"

"When Maggie wasn't back that evening, I set off to retrace her route. Well, at first, I went to the guards and asked if they'd seen her return. None of them had. Then, I tried to speak to a family member to find out what documents they'd given her. After all, they deal with sensitive political and financial matters, and I became concerned she may have carried important documents that had been stolen, or she'd been taken because someone wanted the documents."

"No one from the family would see you?" I gave Hodgepodge a plump piece of cooked damson.

"It was late, and they weren't interested, so I went looking for her. I got to the first drop-off point, the Black Swan Tavern, and they said they'd been expecting Maggie, but she didn't arrive. I asked if there'd been any problems on the road or if anyone had reported people being robbed, and they said no."

"You didn't believe them?" I asked.

"Maggie is careful. She knows how the world works and that it's not all sparkling spells of goodness and everyone getting their happily-ever-afters. It's why she carries an enchanted blade." Gwit waggled his fingers in the air. "Don't worry. She keeps it concealed, but when she's out on her own, I need to ensure she's safe. We practiced with the blade until she was confident using it. If anyone had gone after her, they'd regret it. That blade always finds its mark."

"What did you do after that?" I asked.

"I kept searching. I continued along the route Maggie traveled and went to the next drop-off point. The main relay station for collecting new documents. Again, they hadn't seen her. They'd been expecting her, but she didn't show. I got the same answer at the Rhubarb Café. Her final stop."

"And that was when you became worried and thought she'd been taken?"

His expression tightened. "I know for a fact several families have lost loved ones, and they've never been returned."

"Do the women that go missing fit a particular profile?" Hodgepodge asked.

Gwit's brow furrowed again, and he dabbed crumbs off his lips. "I don't know the details about all of them, but the ones I know of are all under thirty. They come from families with little power or influence, and none of them are married. And, if they're anything like Maggie, they need money."

"There's a pattern," I murmured. "Whoever is taking these women is after a particular type."

"For what reason?" Gwit asked.

I stuffed a big piece of pie in my mouth so I wouldn't have to answer. The book Astrid gave me had detailed the requirements for a successful blood sacrifice to resurrect dragons. It hadn't mentioned age limits, appearance, or prosperity, but perhaps whoever was taking them had more information, so knew who to target.

"Are you still asking around?" Gwit said. "People have started keeping away from me because all I do is ask about Maggie."

"I am, but I've not found much useful information. I'm not giving up, though."

He finished his pie and patted my hand. "Thanks, Bell. I'm glad you're a friend. If I can do anything in return, let me know."

"The pie was more than enough. And you were right, it's delicious. I'm coming here again." I fed the final piece of pie crust to Hodgepodge.

"I should get back to work," Gwit said. "And I need to make a quick stop to pick up a new set of tongs."

"Me too. I need to see what mess the chamber is in after our last set of visitors."

He left us to collect his tongs, and I walked slowly back to the castle, my stomach deliciously full but my thoughts a whirl.

"I know what you're thinking," Hodgepodge said. "You want to save all those women, don't you?"

"So do you. We must figure out where they are and how to set them free."

"Assuming they're even alive."

I walked in silence for a moment. "If it's someone high up doing this, they won't let the women go because they'll talk, and the family will get into trouble for abducting people and bleeding them."

"Which is why they're probably not alive," Hodgepodge said. "Even more reason for us to stay out of this."

I dodged past a noisy street vendor selling cute earthenware pots. "Are you okay with walking around with this knowledge and doing nothing about it?"

Hodgepodge huffed in my ear. "I don't want you to become one of the dead women."

"Allegedly dead. And I won't, providing we're careful." I had no plan to solve this problem, but I'd figure something out.

The rest of the afternoon and evening were spent in a blur of cleaning and thinking. I hadn't come to any conclusions by the time midnight rolled around and I could stagger home, exhaustion clouding my head and making my bones ache.

"We need a quiet night in and some coziness," Hodgepodge said as I finally got through my front door and closed it behind me.

I nodded as I made hot cocoa and then stoked the fire. I tilted my head. "Did you hear that?"

"I heard our bed calling. Heat a brick and put it under the covers to make it extra cozy."

I shook my head. I was certain someone had whispered my name. "I must be exhausted if I'm hearing voices again."

"No reading the dragon book tonight," Hodgepodge said. "The sooner we get it out of here, the better."

I didn't disagree with him. "Tomorrow is our day off, so we can fix everything. And I know just the wise person to talk to about this. Elara will help us."

"After sleep," Hodgepodge said. "No visits to eccentric woodland witches until you've napped."

I kissed his head. "After sleep, we're going on a road trip."

Chapter 10

"We can still turn back before anyone recognizes us." Hodgepodge was tucked into a small pack on my back, with an opening at the top for air and so I could hear him grumble at me.

I pulled my plain brown cloak hood closer to my face and kept my head down. "Nobody knows us outside of the castle walls."

"They'll recognize you're a stranger, though. And they'll be interested when you ask questions about Maggie and what they know about her going missing."

"I'll use a fake name and keep the questions brief." I hurried toward the waiting automobile carriage. They were strange devices operated through a combination of steam and magic. They weren't always comfortable if you picked a seat with broken springs, but they were cheap and meant our journey retracing Maggie's steps could be done in a single morning.

It was my day off from cleaning the stone chamber, but I didn't want anyone to notice I was gone for too long, in case questions were asked.

"Don't talk to anyone unless you have to," Hodgepodge whispered. "And don't look anyone in the eyes, either. Behave subserviently."

"Don't I always?" I muttered.

We waited in the short queue as people boarded the automobile, then I paid my fare and eased into a seat, being careful to sit forward so I didn't squash Hodgepodge.

The view out of the window showed the road busy with travelers visiting the castle, workers coming and going, and tradespeople hurrying past in the chilly gray morning. Although I'd often dreamt of a quiet life in the countryside, I'd miss this hustle and bustle. It made me feel alive to be in the middle of everything happening around the castle.

The automobile lurched to life and took us along the main route, stopping now and again to let more passengers on or some off. We'd gotten up early to make the journey, and my eyes felt heavy as the rhythmic rocking of the automobile encouraged me to sleep. I needed to stay alert. This wasn't the time to sleep on the job.

Twenty minutes later, the Black Swan Tavern came into view, set proud against the side of the road. It was a large, white-painted building, and the double front doors were already open to welcome visitors, despite the early hour.

"This is us," I said.

The elderly sour-faced woman seated beside me gave me a strange look.

I ducked my head. "Sorry, I need to get off."

She shuffled her legs to the side, and I squeezed past and hurried to the door. A few seconds later, we were off the automobile and standing in front of the Black Swan Tavern. Gwit had told us this was the first place Maggie visited on her collection route.

I glanced over my shoulder. The castle stood proudly behind us in the distance. It was the only place I'd ever lived. My mother had worked at the castle, so I was raised there. It felt so strange to question their rule, but I couldn't ignore my growing doubts. At the heart of the Ithric Realm, something was rotten.

"Go in and ask the questions," Hodgepodge whispered. "If you keep lurking and gaping at everything, you'll be marked as an outsider. People won't talk to you."

"I'm going, I'm going," I muttered. I entered the tavern and discovered a bright, welcoming entrance hall. To the left was a sign stating it was a family room, and to the right was the main tavern. I headed in that direction and pushed open the door. There were wide, dark beams running across the ceiling and a bar to the left of the entrance.

There were a few patrons sitting around with early morning refreshments, and one or two people had mugs of coffee and a breakfast in front of them.

I headed to the bar and nodded at the white-haired woman standing behind it.

"What'll it be?" she asked.

"I'm looking for someone," I said. "She passed through recently. She was collecting documents."

"If you want to ask questions, you need to order something."

I had little money on me, so I picked the cheapest item. "Lavender cordial, please."

She grunted and fixed my drink.

I nodded my thanks and took a sip. "Do you know Maggie Buckleberry?"

The woman tidied menus and checked the stock of cider. "I get a lot of people passing through. What does she look like?"

"Maggie is twenty. Short, attractive, with dark shoulder-length hair and a big laugh. This was one of her regular delivery routes. She picked up and dropped off documents for the Ithric family."

The woman's gaze flicked my way. "If she works there, why don't you ask them about her?"

"I would, but they're not easy to talk to," I said. "And I'm hardly in a position to question the family."

"I imagine not." She inspected my frayed brown cloak. "I don't know her. I mind my business when it comes to that family. You'd be wise to do the same."

"You really don't remember Maggie?" I pressed. "She'd only been doing this route for a few weeks before she went missing."

The woman's head jerked up. "Missing! Why would you think she's missing?"

"Because no one has seen her for a long time."

"She probably moved on. So should you." The woman bustled off to serve another customer.

I looked around and saw a couple of servers at the back. I asked them the same questions about Maggie, but they were tight-lipped and unwilling to answer me.

"We need to hurry," Hodgepodge whispered. "The next automobile pulls up in a few minutes. We don't want to wait around for another half an hour if we miss it."

I headed to the door and looked back at the bar. The white-haired woman was watching me with suspicion in her eyes. I hurried out and joined the queue waiting for the automobile, and a few minutes later, we were back on the road.

I desperately wanted to talk things over with Hodgepodge, but I couldn't be seen muttering to myself. If I didn't draw any attention to myself, we'd get away with going on this adventure.

The journey took over an hour before we arrived at the relay station. The building was squat and bland, with a steady stream of people going in and out to send their messages or pick up communications.

I had to queue before I could see anyone. When I reached the front, I was confronted by a gruff-faced man with a large bushy beard and even bushier eyebrows.

"Dropping off or collecting?" he asked.

"Collecting answers," I said. "I need a minute of your time. I'm looking for someone who used to run messages for the Ithric family. Her name is Maggie Buckleberry."

"We get a lot of messages coming through for the family. What about her?" The man glanced over my shoulder at the queue.

"This is one of the last places she visited before she went missing," I said. "I'm trying to find out what happened to her."

He glanced at me and then looked away. "Why do you think she's missing?"

"Because no one has seen her. She could be in trouble. She'd only been working for the Ithric family for a few weeks. I'm checking the last places she visited to see if anyone saw her behaving strangely or having trouble with someone. I need to make sure she's not in any harm."

The man leaned closer. "A word of advice. Harm will find you if you keep searching. Move along."

"You know something?" I inched closer.

"I never said that. I don't know this girl, and I don't want to know her. Believe she's moved on and found somewhere better. Now, step aside, I have customers to see to."

I looked around at the shifting, grumbling queue behind me. I turned back to the man. "You remember her, though?"

"No. I don't remember her. Next, please."

I let out a sigh as I stepped to the side. Maggie had always drawn attention. She was pretty and vivacious and enjoyed a giggle and a flirt. She'd have been remembered, so why were these people saying they didn't know her?

I walked back outside, a chilly breeze lifting my hood. I wandered around the side of the building and eased off my backpack, so it was easier to talk to Hodgepodge. "This isn't going as I'd planned."

"We need a break," Hodgepodge said. "The next stop serves food. Before you ask questions, get yourself a slice of pie and a mug of coffee."

That sounded like a great idea. I'd only had a few bites of dried apple before leaving in the morning, and my stomach was grumbling. "I wonder if there's a portal tunnel around here? We could use that to get to the last stop."

I gently rubbed the small tattoo on the inside of my wrist. It hummed softly, suggesting there was a tunnel, but it was a good hour's walk away. "Automobile it is."

We waited out of the wind until the next automobile arrived and clambered on. It was another hour's journey, and I snoozed for a few minutes until my head hit the glass and I woke with a start.

We got to Maggie's final destination and climbed out of the automobile. We headed inside a lively café with a collection point in one corner, which I assumed was where Maggie would have gone, and a seating area on the other side, which was half full of customers.

"Order our pie then go ask your questions," Hodgepodge said.

I went to the counter, ordered a large slice of cherry pie and a mug of coffee, took my order number, then headed to the collection area. There was no one waiting to be served, just a tired-eyed, middle-aged woman flicking through paperwork behind the chipped counter.

She didn't look up as I stopped in front of her. "Picking up or dropping off?"

"Picking up answers."

She glanced at me. "Then you're in the wrong place."

"I'm looking for a friend who's gone missing. Her name is Maggie Buckleberry." I described Maggie. "She's been doing a delivery and collection route for the Ithric family until recently."

"What's that got to do with me?"

"This was the last place she visited. Please, I'm worried about her."

The woman sighed. "Everyone who drops off or collects needs to sign the ledger. Let me check." She grabbed a huge leather-bound book and flipped it open. She held her hands over it, and magic sparked from her palms.

I gasped and stepped back. It was so unusual to see people using magic so openly.

She looked up at me and grinned. "One of the few perks of this job. We're so far from the castle that we can bend the rules. Unless you want me to thumb through these pages to find your friend's name. And that ain't happening."

"No! Any information you have is welcome." I was fascinated by the pink sparks that pinged off the page as she turned them.

"I see why your friend might have disappeared." The woman slammed the ledger shut and placed it back on the shelf.

"What did you find out?" I asked.

"She was supposed to deliver correspondence from the Ithric family and pick up a document to return to them, but she never showed and missed her delivery slot. The document was sitting here for a week before someone else collected it." The woman tutted to herself. "Chances are, the family discovered she wasn't doing her job and fired her. She's scampered away with her tail between her legs. Not that it would have done her any good. Once the family blackballs you, you're done for. May as well turn into a hermit and vanish into the wilderness."

"Maggie never got here?"

"Looks like it."

"You do remember her, though?"

She hesitated then shook her head. "Can't say I do."

"You're sure? The last time you saw her, she wasn't worried about anything?"

"I didn't see her, I don't know her, and I don't want to get involved in whatever you're meddling in." She looked over my shoulder. "Is that your pie?"

I turned and saw a waitress standing by a table, holding a tray with cherry pie and coffee. I raised a hand to get her attention. When I turned back to the counter, the woman had snapped a blind down.

I headed over and settled at a small table, thanking the waitress for my food. I ate several large mouthfuls of pie in greedy gulps, then I took my backpack off and set it on the table. "Hodgie, something strange is going on. Everyone is saying the same thing. It's like they've been coached to lie."

"Or paid to hide the truth," he whispered. "It could be the Ithric family paying them. And if they learn you're snooping, you'll lose more than your job."

"People don't just vanish."

"Untrue. I know spells—"

"Shush. Spells we can't use. Besides, Maggie wouldn't have had access to that kind of magic."

"You're forgetting, she carried an illegal enchanted blade Gwit gave her. Maybe he has more magic up his sleeves that he taught her. That would have brought trouble to her door."

I twisted my mouth to the side. Visiting this final stop only made me more suspicious about what had happened to Maggie. I stuffed another chunk of delicious, sweet pie into my mouth and discreetly fed Hodgepodge a cherry. "Elara will have answers for us."

"Your wise woman friend may be useful. She always has her ear to the ground. I'm surprised she hasn't had them snipped off because she's so nosy."

I chuckled as I finished the pie, savoring it since I'd spent the last of my money on the delicious treat, then stood and settled Hodgepodge onto my back again.

My next stop wasn't to a place Maggie had visited but to a family friend. Elara Soothling lived a hermit-like life in a patch of wild woodland that few visited. She'd been a friend of my late mother's and had consoled me during her untimely death. Since then, she'd checked in on me from time to time to ensure I was doing okay. She'd been old when I'd known her as a child but never seemed to get any older.

I headed out of the café, my belly full and my thoughts focused. "Let's see what our woodland witch has heard about these disappearances."

Chapter 11

The public automobile took me within a twenty-minute walk of Elara's dwelling, and I was happy to stretch my legs and get fresh air, despite how chilly it was, striding away from the main road and along a series of smaller, quieter roads.

It didn't take me long to find the discrete path that led to Elara's thatched woodland home. If you didn't know it was there, you'd never find it. It was carefully concealed behind a copse of overgrown trees, and although Elara never confirmed it, I was certain she used magic to ensure walkers didn't accidentally stumble onto her cottage and nose around where they weren't wanted.

The front door was open when I caught my first glimpse of her home, and I smiled. Elara always knew when I was coming. I hurried to the door, and she appeared, a smile on her wrinkled face as she engulfed me in a mint and thyme-scented hug.

"It's been too long, child." Elara stepped back, keeping hold of my shoulders. She wore her usual jumble of warm, mismatched clothing and a pair of indoor felt boots in a soft shade of lilac.

"It's always so busy at the castle. I promise, I'll visit more often, but the dragons take up so much time."

She clicked her tongue against the roof of her mouth. "And of course, you never want to leave them. Your mother was the same. She adored the dragons. Come in. What brings you out this way?"

I pulled off my backpack and set it down, along with my cloak. Hodgepodge hopped out and trotted over to the waiting bowl of fruit and started eating with gusto.

I sat on the wobbly wooden chair at Elara's rustic kitchen table. "Can't I just want to visit my favorite person?"

Elara chuckled, the sound like a croaky frog. "I'm waiting."

I smiled at her. "You got me. I need your advice. I'm worried about something happening at the castle."

"Go on. You're not in trouble, are you?" Elara stopped her progress across the cluttered but clean kitchen.

"Bell will be in serious trouble if she keeps meddling," Hodgepodge said, his mouth full of ripe apple.

"I'm fine. I'm in no trouble, but I've discovered women who live in the castle and nearby villages are going missing. Thirty in total. There could be more."

"You're sure they're missing?" Elara set a kettle on the hob to boil. Her fingers wrapped around the orange amulet she always wore around her neck.

"I had no idea what was going on at first, but a friend's sister vanished, and he's been looking for her. He's asked for my help, so I've been asking around."

"It sounds like the problem is bigger than some girls losing their way." Elara cocked her head, waiting for me to reveal more.

"I... I've also had others helping me. And I found some worrying clues. Blood on a dragon in the stone chamber, and then I read a book. It details a way to bring the dragons back. It involves blood sacrifice."

Elara pressed a hand against her chest, her fingers still clutching the amulet. "Bell! Don't meddle in such twisted business. And what are you doing reading something like that? How did you even get your hands on it?"

"It's a long story you're better off not knowing," I said. "But now I know what's going on, I can't turn my back on it."

"You could." Hodgepodge's words were muffled by the giant slice of banana he chewed on. Elara always over-indulged his love of sweet fruit.

"It wouldn't feel right. These women are in danger."

"I count you amongst them. You're in danger by learning about this." Elara turned away and sorted through several pots of herbal teas on the counter before selecting one. She placed a bowl and two mugs in front of her, added herbs, and then the boiling water.

"I know you helped my mother when she was investigating the black market trading the Ithric family was involved in," I said. "You know they're untrustworthy. And I believe they're involved in this, too."

Elara turned her head and pressed a finger against her lips. "No talk like that."

"It's true, isn't it? Mother told me about it."

"She was wrong to do so." Elara brought over the mugs and set a water bowl down for Hodgepodge next to his food. She sat in a seat opposite me and stared hard into my eyes. "I admire your courage, but I must advise caution."

I wrapped my fingers around the warm mug. "I am being careful. We traced Maggie's last known movements to see if anyone knew anything that could be useful."

Elara pursed her lips. "That's not careful! Why would you do such a risky thing?"

"I didn't use my name. And I made sure no one saw us leaving the castle."

"Even so, it's dangerous. The family has spies everywhere."

"You'd do the same. You always help people in need."

"And look where it got me! Exiled to the forest. If any member of the Ithric family discovers where I am, this'll be the last place I see. I don't want that for you. You need to be free and safe. You have your whole life ahead of you."

"I don't feel I'm either. And... I don't trust the family. Not anymore. Not after reading that book. What if they're behind the women going missing? They had the book in their private collection, so someone must have read it. And there are rumors they need the dragons back to restore order, so they're getting desperate."

"My dear child, what can you do if they are?" Elara reached over and caught hold of my hand. "I don't say that to be cruel, but you have a safe life. You have a good job working in the castle and a home. And I know you love those dragons. Why stir things and risk losing everything you have?"

I lifted my mug with my free hand and took a sip. The herbs were flavorful, and there was a hint of honey mixed in them. I took another sip. "I've always opted for a quiet life, but maybe that was wrong. I should do more."

"This is all rumors and speculation. They'll get you in trouble," Elara said.

"The book suggests it's the truth. And since that book was owned by the Ithric family—"

Elara sucked in a breath. "You stole it from the family?"

"No! Well, I took something that was stolen by someone else. She told me I needed to read the book if I wanted to learn the truth."

Elara shook her head vigorously. "This gets worse. Your mother would be spinning in her grave if she hadn't been burned at the stake."

"I'm sure her ashes are swirling with displeasure," I murmured. "I also know she'd want justice for these women."

Elara was silent for a moment. It wasn't an uncomfortable silence, and I was happy to sit and sip tea and be enveloped in the comforting warmth of Elara's quirky home.

"This calls for snacks." Elara stood and brought out a plate of cookies packed with dark chocolate chunks. "We'll sit, drink, and consider your options. Find a safe way through for both of you. Hodgepodge, you're at as much risk as Bell. Don't think Lady Isolda won't turn you into a purse if she catches you."

He hissed. "Ach! I'll become a haunted purse and bite her in the butt if she makes such a mistake."

I took a cookie and bit into it. As expected, it was delicious. Elara always made the best cookies. "That's why I'm here. I want to figure out how to fix this."

Elara quirked a white eyebrow. "You want my advice?"

I nodded.

"You know too much, and that's dangerous. I promised your mother I'd keep you safe."

"And you have. You've always cautioned me to be careful. My life is a big bubble of careful. I never take any risks."

"Yet I didn't caution you enough because here you are, sitting at my table, telling me of your quest to solve a problem the family has made. My girl, when was the last time you cast a spell?"

"I had to speed clean the stone chamber recently." I sat straight and flexed my fingers.

She smiled indulgently. "A spell with power. One that makes the hairs on the back of your neck tingle and your eyes burn. Because if you're going up against the Ithric family, you'll have to use extreme magic to defeat them. Dark, twisted, ruinous magic to end their stranglehold on the realm."

A churning sensation slid through my gut. "I never talked about defeating them."

"If you expose what they're doing and you're right that they're taking women for a blood sacrifice, what do you think will happen? People will nod in approval of the family taking their loved ones? There'll be a revolution. The Ithric dynasty will come under attack, and in return, they'll target those who started this. And you're right in the middle."

Hodgepodge wandered over and snuggled into my lap. He flopped down, his eyes half shut.

I rested a hand on his head, my stomach still churning. "What should I do?"

Elara took a cookie but didn't eat it. "Do you trust any of the royal guards?"

"Not really. Why should I? They're loyal to the family. If they know anything, they won't reveal it to me."

"Is there no one on the inside of any influence who can help you?"

I thought about it for a few seconds then shook my head. "I'm a servant. I'm powerless."

"Then you've answered your dilemma. The best you can do is put out a discreet word for people to be careful. Although it sounds like word is already getting out that women are going missing, so people will be taking care. Do you know if there's a type? Do the women have anything in common?"

I nodded. "There's a pattern. I could spread the gossip through the grapevine, but will that be enough?"

"If that's all you can do, then that's enough," Elara said.

She was right, but why did it feel wrong? How could I, a cleaner with no renown, no connections, and very little influence, make more of a difference?

I ate more treats and finished my herbal tea as I mulled over this problem. I looked down at Hodgepodge. He was fast asleep. The traveling must have tired him out. I stifled a yawn behind my hand.

"You're welcome to stay the night," Elara said. "You won't get back until dark."

"Thanks, but I don't like to be away from the castle for too long. This is a deviation from my usual routine, so I don't want people noticing."

"Good thinking. Stick to what you know. It's the safest path."

I sighed. "Maybe you're right. I'll get the word out and see if we can get women walking with a friend or family member when they're outside, so they're less vulnerable. The girl I'm looking for was taken along this route. Although it was hard to get useful information out of anyone. I was warned off, and then they denied ever having seen or known Maggie. I don't think they were telling the truth."

Elara collected the mugs and plate and took them to the sink. She set them down and kept her back to me. "I'm sorry, child. I wish things could be different."

"It's not so bad working at the castle. And I'll make more effort to visit."

"I don't mean that. I wish you hadn't come here and told me what you know."

"I won't get you in trouble. I was careful like I always am when coming here." My words slurred, and my eyes were so heavy I could barely keep them open.

I blinked slowly as Elara approached me. Panic tingled up my spine, but my legs and arms were too heavy for me to move. The last thing I remembered was Elara putting her arm around my shoulders.

※※※※ ※※※※

I jerked awake, my head banging against something cold and hard. I drew in a breath and winced. My throat was dry, my eyes gritty, and my head pounded. I looked around at my unfamiliar surroundings. It was cold and gloomy, and the floor I was lying on was hard, damp stone.

I rolled onto my back and groaned. Everything ached. I stayed still, attempting to get my bearings. The last thing I remembered was talking to Elara.

My heart sank as I detected a bitter aftertaste in my mouth. She'd betrayed me. The herbal tea must have been spiked. She hadn't taken a sip of whatever she'd brewed for us. Why? We were friends. More than friends, she felt like family.

"Hodgepodge?" The word grated out of my dry mouth. I felt around for him, but he wasn't there.

That got me moving. I sat up, ignoring the room swaying, and looked around. I was in a small cell, the walls and floor stone, and a barred door in front of me. I staggered to the door, scraping my knees through my skirt, and attempted to open it. No surprise, it was locked.

I peered into the gloomy corridor. Though I'd never been down here before, I had to assume this was the castle dungeon. How did I get here? Did Elara bring me? Was she working for the Ithric family? She despised them and had always been suspicious that they'd had something to do with my mother's death, although nothing had been proven.

"Hodgepodge?" I whispered into the gloom. "Where are you?"

There was no reply, no skittering of claws across stone, no puffs of smoke. Tears clogged my throat. He'd been found and taken. If Elara had handed us over to the Ithric family, Hodgepodge wouldn't survive. They loathed difference. And Hodgepodge was wonderfully unique.

I rested my head against the bars and closed my eyes. I wouldn't panic. There had to be a way out. Maybe Elara hadn't betrayed me, but somehow, agents from the family had found her and she was trapped here, too. But why drug me? It had to be her. It made no sense.

I stayed where I was, taking deep breaths and getting my panic under control. The sound of soft crying reached my ears, and I squinted into the dense grayness. "Hello? Who's there?"

The crying stopped then started again a few seconds later.

"Can you hear me? Does anyone know how I got down here? Please, I need help."

"We all need help," a female whisper came from the darkness.

"Who's that?"

"Stop talking. We're not supposed to talk to each other. The guards hate it."

I looked around, trying to locate the source of the voice. "Who are you?"

On the other side of the corridor, a pale face appeared behind another barred door. It was a young woman with tangled black hair and a pale face. Dirt was smeared on one cheek.

I raised a hand. "I'm Bell. Are you... okay?"

"Hardly. And you'll look like this soon enough after you've been down here a couple of months and they've half-drained your blood," the woman said.

My body shook. "How did I get here?"

"You were brought in the same as all of us. You were unconscious, and there was a bag over your head. Two guards dragged you in and dumped you into the cell. Welcome. This is your new home."

"I don't remember any of that. I was meeting with a friend, and then..."

"And then you woke here. We've all got the same story. We got tricked or drugged or knocked out or lied to. It all ends up the same way."

"Who are you?"

"The same as you. A dead woman walking."

I studied the woman. She was thin, her skin grubby, and her complexion looked almost translucent. She was deathly pale, and there were bruises on her flesh. I pressed my lips together. It was all true. There were women being held in the dungeons.

"They take your blood for the dragons?" I asked.

"You know something about that?" she finally said, after glaring at me until I grew uneasy.

"I'm learning something new every day," I said. "I don't recognize you. You don't work at the castle."

"I live in the next village. That's where they grabbed me. Two friendly guys who wanted to buy me a drink and sweet talk me."

Someone shushed us, but the woman waved them away.

"How long have you been here?" I asked.

"A month? Maybe more. Time gets meaningless when there's nothing to do but wait."

"We can't stay here!" I tugged at the bars.

"Unless you've got some miracle to get us out, that's exactly what we're doing."

My tongue traced across my dry lips. "How many of you are down here?"

"It doesn't matter. There could be a thousand of us, but we're still powerless."

I refused to believe that. "Did you see a small lizard when I was brought in? He's my companion."

"Lizard? No, and they wouldn't let you keep him with you. They've probably roasted him. The guards are barbarians."

I shook my head, not accepting that outcome. I fished into my underskirt pockets and pulled out a magic twist. It was old, but the magic should be stable. I used it to clear piles of rubbish, so there might be enough power in it to blow open the door. Maybe. I'd never tried my magic on metal bars.

"I wouldn't do that if I were you," the woman said. "If the family catches you using magic, they'll kill you."

I hesitated, the magic twist squeezed in my palm. I'd always wanted a quiet life with no drama. I should have listened to Hodgepodge when he warned me that doing this would get me in trouble.

The woman's gaze flashed to the side, and she vanished. A second later, footsteps approached. I backed away, my heart in my throat. It was Warwick, Prince Godric, and two armed guards, carrying their trademark sparking sticks. I shrank back into the shadows, turning my face away so they wouldn't see me.

"She'll do," Prince Godric's voice rang out. "Take her away. You know what to do."

My heart bounced against my chest as keys jangled and a door opened. There was a soft whimpering as a woman was taken out of her cell, her pleas ignored as she was shackled.

"This is going too slowly," Prince Godric said. "All of these women are useless. We must expand the search, broaden it out to more villages and towns. The right one is out there."

"If we take more, people will grow suspicious." Warwick's voice was a low grumble.

"Let the idiots be suspicious. And stop helping her. She's capable of walking."

I risked a glance. Warwick had his hand under the woman's elbow as she swayed on her feet.

"The last one fell down the stairs, sir."

"Which proved she wasn't worthy of being a part of this incredible journey," Prince Godric said, "You're too softhearted, Warwick. It'll be your undoing. Remember what happened to your brother?"

There was a heartbeat of silence. "It's hardly something I could forget."

"He was weak-willed and pathetic. That got him killed. Don't be like him. Focus on the mission. Get me more girls. Strong ones. Not like this sop."

Warwick lowered his head and removed his hand from the woman's elbow.

"Take another one, too. Maybe we need more blood," Prince Godric said. "The dragons must be feeling greedy. They want a proper show of deference."

The coldness in his tone made my stomach clench. Prince Godric hated the dragons. He was only trying to bring them back because he was getting desperate about losing his chance to sit in the royal power seat his mother occupied.

Another woman was taken out of her cell, and the guards led them away.

"Let's get out of here. This place stinks." Prince Godric marched away.

Warwick turned, and his gaze met mine. His eyes widened as I shrank away. He said nothing and followed Prince Godric.

I sank to my knees and closed my eyes. I'd blown it. I'd lost Hodgepodge, my job, and potentially my life. I stayed on my knees for fifteen minutes, determined not to cry but having to blink every few seconds to stop the tears from falling.

Soft footsteps had me alert and crouching, ready to do I didn't know what, but I wasn't going down without a fight.

Warwick loomed into view, his expression so fierce my knees trembled. He unlocked my cell door without saying a word.

I backed up until I hit the wall. "I'm not going. I won't be drained like the other women. I'm no use to you. You don't need me."

He arched an eyebrow and gestured me to follow him with one finger. "Let's move."

"Where?"

"If you keep asking questions, you'll give me no choice but to leave you behind. You've seen what happens to the people here. So, what will it be?"

Chapter 12

I kept my head up as I followed Warwick out of my cell and into the main stone corridor. I looked into each cell we passed. There were twenty in total. Many of the inhabitants were hunched at the back, their faces turned away, but I could see at least two women occupied each cell.

"Where are you taking me?" I asked.

Warwick didn't respond.

Fear fizzled down my spine, making my nerves tingle and the tips of my fingers go numb. I could run. I was fast on my feet and small. Warwick was a wall of solid muscle, so maybe that would slow him. But if he caught me, there'd be nothing left of me.

I kept looking around, hopeful to see Hodgepodge. Where would they put him? Not in a cell. He'd be able to slip through the bars. Maybe in a cage. I had to get him back. If I found out they'd done anything to hurt him...

I grabbed a sharp piece of stone from the floor and hurried closer to Warwick.

"Don't even think about doing anything that stupid." Warwick's voice grumbled out of his broad chest.

I lowered the hand I had raised. I couldn't outfight him with brute strength. "I wasn't doing anything."

"Your footsteps changed, your breathing grew faster, and I heard the stone scrape as you lifted it. Follow me. And drop your weapon if you know what's good for you."

I scowled at his back and flung the stone to the floor. We reached a set of stone steps that went down. I had no idea there was a lower level beneath the dungeon.

Warwick led the way, not bothering to glance over his shoulder since he appeared to have supernatural powers that meant he knew what I was doing without looking. Maybe he did. The royal guards had more freedom to use magic, as the sparking staff in his hand showed.

We reached a solid stone wall, and he pressed his hand against it. There was a small glow from beneath his palm, and a doorway appeared.

"You use the servants' tunnels?" I asked.

"Of course. And I know you do." He stepped inside, clicked his fingers, and light filled the corridor.

I hesitated at the entrance. "Is this route taking me to another dungeon? One worse than the one above our heads?"

"That's the only castle dungeon." He finally turned and met my gaze. Rather than anger burning in his eyes, I was surprised to see curiosity. "What are you waiting for?"

"I'm buying a few more minutes of life. I fear if I go in there, I'm never coming out."

A flicker of a smile crossed his face, but it was gone just as quickly. "You'll live so long as you don't get any more dumb thoughts about attacking me."

"You're taking me to my certain doom. A woman has a right to defend herself."

Warwick smirked. "Against me? Good luck. But you won't meet a certain doom in here. I have questions, that's all."

I looked over my shoulder. Going back up those steps and into the dungeon would get me nowhere. I turned back to Warwick and stepped into the tunnel. The door sealed behind me. "Where does this lead?"

"It connects with the main routes. If you go straight ahead, you'll get outside, eventually. But I didn't bring you here to talk about the servants' tunnels. Tell me what you know."

"Um... I could give you a list of ingredients to make a cleaning solution that'll fix any stain. That's my specialty."

"I'm not interested in your job. Although it gives you unlimited access to the stone dragons."

"That's what I'm paid to do. I look after their chamber," I replied.

"I know all about you," Warwick said. "You talk to the dragons. You even sing to them. It's pleasant."

Color heated my cheeks. "Oh! I never see you around the stone chamber."

"I'm always around. It's my job to pay attention to any threats that may harm the family."

"Then if you're looking at me, you're doing a lousy job."

"I'm not so sure about that. You have a connection to the dragons."

"No. I mean, I wish they were here. I'm always hopeful they'll return, but I have no special link to them. There aren't any dragons in the realm to connect with. Not that I'd know how to do that. When they were here, I admired them from a distance."

Warwick shook his head. "It's more than that. No one treats them the way you do. People visit them and leave offerings, but you treat them like friends."

I huffed out a breath. "I don't know what else to tell you. Since you've been watching me, which, if I may say, is creepy and will get you a big old stalker badge to pin to your chest, you know what I do. I start work at dawn, ensure the stone chamber is clean, and then repair the damage the visitors do. I stay until midnight."

"And on your day off?"

"I usually read, eat, and sleep."

"Not recently."

I lifted my eyebrows. "You've been following me everywhere?"

"I didn't have to. The castle's connections spread far across the realm. Don't think that, when you're outside the walls, you're free to do as you choose."

"The family has spies everywhere," I muttered.

"Something like that."

"If you see everything, you'll know where Hodgepodge is." It was a risk to mention him, but Warwick must know what happened to him.

"Your creature?" he asked. "It's an unusual choice of companion."

"Hodgepodge is loyal, supportive, and he helps me. What more could I ask for?"

"He's also unsanctioned by the family. No magical companion animals allowed. And I know that one has something a little special about him."

"You think I don't know that? It's why I keep him concealed when anyone from the family is around."

"In that odd skirt." His gaze flicked over my clothing.

"There's nothing odd about a practical skirt with numerous pockets."

"I'll take your word for that."

"Well? What happened to him?"

"I wasn't here when you were brought in. I suspect he was killed."

My throat tightened, and I pressed a fisted hand against my stomach. "I'd know if he was dead."

"How would that be? You're using illegal magic to bond with him like witches do with their familiars?"

"No! But when you have a close bond with someone, you know when something bad has happened to them."

"Is that so? Sounds like unnatural trickery to me."

"You must have people you're close to."

"Can't say I do. It's the best way to be." Warwick glanced away for a second. "The family despises difference, and your creature is an oddity they won't tolerate."

"Hodgepodge is perfect. Give him back."

"I don't have him."

"Then find out who does."

Warwick arched a brow. "You're hardly in a position to give me orders."

"I wish I had thrown that stone at your head. Made you sorry. And I will get Hodgepodge back."

"I look forward to seeing you try." Warwick opened his mouth as if to say more then snapped it shut.

"Why have you brought me down here? You could have left me in that cell, so Prince Godric used me just like the other women he's holding against their will," I said.

"What do you think he's using them for?"

I pressed my lips together, refusing to let my anger make me slip and reveal what I knew.

Warwick waited. So did I.

"I admire your passion and dedication to the dragons." Warwick drew in a slow breath. "If the family had shown the same commitment, we'd still have them, and there would be no chaos to deal with. Many lives have been lost since the dragons were taken from us."

"Like your brother?"

His teeth flashed. "What do you know about him?"

"Nothing! I just overheard... it's nothing." I stared at him. "The way you're talking makes me think you don't approve of the Ithric family."

"My loyalty is to them."

"You condone that they're abducting and imprisoning women?"

He half-turned in the corridor, his head brushing the ceiling. "I've said too much. But you don't deserve to be in a cell. You do good work for the dragons. You're loyal to them."

"I won't be anymore. Once the family learns I've been locked in the dungeon, my job is finished. And that'll be the best outcome of this dreary situation." I reached forward to touch his arm but then lowered my hand. "Warwick, you must know what they're doing is wrong. You can't support this."

He rested his hands flat on the stone wall and closed his eyes. "They have to bring the dragons back. It's for the good of everyone."

"Abduction, illegal imprisonment, and hurting innocent people won't do that. Dragons won't thrive under such behavior."

"What if it's the only option?" He glanced at me, and there was indecision in his eyes. I'd never seen Warwick look indecisive in his life.

"What about the upcoming royal marriage? The family is convinced a baby will soon follow. Camilla could be our savior."

He snorted. "That won't happen. They're living in a fairy tale if they think the union will bring forth children. There have been no children born for years."

"Camilla comes from a different realm. She's supposed to bring good fortune and prosperity."

"You got the prosperous bit right. But the union isn't happy. I've passed her chamber at night and heard her crying."

"Oh. I had heard..."

Warwick gestured for me to continue. "What have the gossips been saying about her?"

"The families made a deal, using Camilla as a bargaining chip. They bargained her hand in marriage for trade routes."

"There are a few more details to add. You won't have heard that Lady Isolda tricked Camilla's family into ensuring this marriage went ahead, even when they got the raw end of the deal," Warwick said. "And an unhappy marriage will mean there's no chance of a child, especially when the dragons cursed this realm for what the family did to them."

My eyebrows shot up. "You know that for a fact?"

"It depends on which version of the truth you listen to." Warwick pushed away from the wall.

"How can you support Prince Godric?" I asked. "I heard him talk to you. He's cruel. He made fun of you for helping a woman and said you were soft-hearted."

"He's an asshat of the worst order."

Surprised laughter shot out of my mouth. "I've never heard you talk badly about a member of the family."

"I know better than to do it in front of people who can't keep secrets. You should learn from me." He gestured between us. "This was a mistake."

"I disagree. I'm learning a lot. I figured you'd brought me here to kill me or exile me. But now you're asking me questions about the dragons and telling me you don't approve of Prince Godric. I don't understand, but I like what I'm hearing."

"You don't need to understand it all. But know this. Sometimes, I won't let bad things happen to good people."

"Will it stay that way? The guards must have seen me brought into the dungeon. They know I'm here."

"They report and answer to me."

It wasn't the answer I hoped for, but a little of the fear dancing around my stomach faded. Maybe I'd get out of this alive. "Is Prince Godric responsible for the blood I found on Stormwing?"

Warwick whirled toward me so fast that I gasped and stepped back. "Say that again."

I swallowed my fear. "That's what got me curious. It was just before Prince Jasper and Camilla came to visit the stone chamber. I did a final check to make sure it was perfect for their visit, and I found a smear of blood on a dragon's flank. Not a small smear."

Warwick glared at a spot above my head. "The idiot's become reckless. I knew he was doing it, but I couldn't confront him. He said he was taking the women for his bed chamber, but it was a lie. He takes them to the dragons and locks himself in with them, reeking of dark magic and madness. No one else is allowed to see what goes on."

I drew in a deep breath. "What's he doing once he's with the dragons?"

"He's only supposed to make small offerings in a blessed chalice to them, not smear blood all over them! Idiot."

"I prefer asshat. I saw no chalice, just a large smear of blood."

Warwick hissed air between his teeth. "He'll get caught. Lady Isolda doesn't approve of the sacrifices. She still thinks she can make changes without resurrecting the dragons. She doesn't want them back."

"The family is fighting over them?"

"Lady Isolda has a heart of stone, and Prince Godric was born with madness seeping through his veins. It's a toxic mix. Bring the two together and they clash like lightning bolts. Prince Jasper is a weakling. Lord Crosby is insane, and the rest of the family is kept at arm's length or confined to the turrets, so they have no say over what goes on."

"It's definitely Prince Godric working alone? I haven't seen him in the chamber regularly."

"You only care for the place until midnight. That's when he lurks around. But he's getting desperate if he's taking the women and bleeding them so blatantly. Fool! He believes the old myths."

"From the book?"

Warwick's eyes narrowed, and the glare he fixed me with felt like it pierced my chest and went straight to my heart. "What do you know about the book taken from the collection room?"

I shook my head rapidly. "Old myths are often written down. I never took Prince Godric for a big reader, but perhaps, when he was bored, he picked up a book and read... something."

Warwick chuffed out a laugh. "How did you do it? You couldn't have been working alone to get into the collection room without getting caught."

I pressed my lips together and shook my head again. I wasn't getting my friends in trouble because of my indiscretion.

His chuckle was low as he ran a hand through his hair. "You surprise me, Bell. Few people do that. I assumed when the collection room was broken into, it was the work of a master thief, and they took the book, the coins, and the ring to order."

I opened my eyes wider and feigned innocence.

"But it was you. Do you still have the book?"

I shrugged. I had to get that book out from under my mattress.

"Read it. Every page. You'll see why Prince Godric is becoming reckless and desperate. He believes the sacrifices need to be fresh." Warwick grimaced. "He's out of his mind. You can't bring back the dead."

It was time to make a choice. Warwick hadn't brought me here to destroy me. Or maybe this was a ruse, and it was his way of interrogating me to get answers for the family, and then he'd hand me over to them. But I sensed something about him, a desire for change and an absolute disgust for Prince Godric. I was about to do something either very brave or very foolish.

"I plan on helping those women and stopping Prince Godric. I know about his plans. And I know he wants the dragons back by making blood sacrifices. It's wrong." The words came out of me in a rush.

Warwick stared at me, unblinking. "What are you going to do about it?"

"Whatever it takes. And you know now, so arrest me or let me leave and do my best to change things."

He exhaled slowly, a series of emotions flicking across his face. "Go to work. I have things to think about."

Chapter 13

I'd been in a state of low-level panic ever since Warwick took me back up the stone steps, past the cells, and into the castle. He hadn't spoken, simply gestured for me to get out of his sight.

I wasn't sure I was out of danger. Would he report me? He'd told me he was loyal to the Ithric family but had spouted hatred for Prince Godric. And he didn't believe what the book said. The dragons couldn't be brought back with sacrifice.

My mind was a whirl of confusion as I buzzed through my checks of the stone chamber before the visitors arrived and the daily grind began. Why had Warwick let me out of the cell and told me so much? Wasn't he worried I'd go to the family and reveal what he'd told me? He was as vulnerable as I was.

Once I'd completed this first cleaning shift, I had a mission to accomplish. I was finding Hodgepodge. Warwick was wrong. He wasn't dead. And since Prince Godric was involved, the chances were, he'd trapped Hodgepodge somewhere, and it wouldn't be anywhere nice. I had fifty minutes to find him before my absence was noticed when the chamber didn't get cleaned.

I dashed along the corridor, pausing now and again to fake clean as I searched every nook and cranny for Hodgepodge. The benefit of being one of the lowest-status servants in the castle was that most people barely noticed me. I was a shadow in the corner of their vision as they went about their important work, so I could search the corridors and rooms on the lower level with no one asking questions. And if they did notice me, they saw a nameless, meek servant cleaning up after everybody. It was the perfect disguise.

I stopped by the grand staircase. It was an enormous broad expanse of wood with a rich red carpet running up the middle. I had to go to the upper levels, and that brought with it a greater risk. The upper levels were for the important people. Those who served the family in matters of political, military, and economic value. Go up one more level, and you'd find the exclusive family quarters. The bedrooms, the dressing chambers, the luxurious bathrooms. I'd only been up there once to clean the fireplace in Prince Godric's chambers when his usual maid was sick.

The servants' tunnels would get me most of the way. But once I was at the upper level, I'd be exposed, and there'd be no way I could talk myself out of why I was up there. The family kept a small, tight-knit group of yes-people around them, and I was as far from that group as possible.

But this was for Hodgepodge. I wasn't leaving him in Prince Godric's twisted clutches. I was getting him out and making sure he was safe.

I placed a few cleaning products in a bucket, stored the rest of my supplies in the closet, and then accessed the tunnels. I hurried along, ascending the first set of rough stone steps to the next level. It was early, barely past dawn, so the place was quiet, coolness in the air as I crept along the corridors. Most of these rooms were kept as offices or storage, so it was simple to check each one without being noticed. I whispered Hodgepodge's name into every room, but he didn't reply.

It took half an hour to check the rooms, and I was uncomfortably aware I was running out of time. Visitors would be in the chamber by now. I stopped by the next set of grand steps. The family never rose early, and their wait staff and servants would just be stirring. I looked around, took a risk, and dashed up the plush red carpet.

I reached the top level and stopped in front of an enormous oil painting depicting Lady Isolda and her husband, Lord Crosby Ithric. He'd been locked in the west turret for over a decade. Apparently, he'd shown signs of madness and, for his own safety, was kept in there. I'd never seen him, although I'd heard plenty about him. Mad Lord Crosby. Lady Isolda had caught him dancing naked under a full moon and chanting to the dragons. Many people whispered he was dead and Lady Isolda put on a show by visiting him once a week, when, in truth, his body had been tossed out of a high window and then dragged away to an unmarked grave somewhere in the castle grounds.

The painting showed him to be a handsome man, with warm brown eyes, the opposite of Lady Isolda's icy, indifferent glare.

I tiptoed along the corridor. I had to check each room, but I needed to be silent. I tucked my cleaning bucket under a side table and reached the first room. I eased the handle down, pushed the door open, and peered inside. It was a dressing chamber. The curtains were drawn over the window, letting little light in.

"Hodgepodge?"

No reply.

When I found him, perhaps it would be time to leave the castle for good. I'd suggest it to him. He'd mentioned Crimson Cove. It would be a different world, a different way of living, but we'd be protected by the angels, and I could get to know Finn, the intriguing angel-demon I'd met a few times. We could be safe there.

I sighed and shook my head. This place had always been my home, and I had friends here, but was that enough of a reason to stay if the Ithric family considered us enemies? I continued my creep along the corridor but stopped at the sound of muffled voices.

No, not muffled voices, whispers, and they were coming from the walls.

I pressed my ear against the nearest wall.

"Keep going. So close."

I jerked back and stared at the wall. Who was on the other side?

"Be careful."

Was I imagining things? Was this a side effect of whatever Elara had drugged me with?

"Hodgepodge! Find him."

"I'm trying!" I looked all around the corridor. "Where is he?"

"Keep going. Close. Next corridor. Third door on the right."

What the heck! How did this weird disembodied voice know where Hodgepodge was being kept?

Whether this was a figment of my drug-hazed imagination or a castle ghost who wanted to be helpful, I wasn't taking the assistance for granted. I hurried along the corridor and stopped by a door the voice told me to check. My blood chilled and my throat tightened. Prince Godric's voice drifted closer. It was coming from these chambers.

I debated whether to risk going in when footsteps sounded on the stairs. I opened the door and slid inside, easing it almost closed. Two guards patrolled past the door a moment later. If I'd waited a second longer, they'd have caught me and I'd have been hauled back to the dungeon.

I gently closed the door and turned around. It was a luxurious entrance room with a gilded mirror on the wall and thick carpet underfoot. It was the gateway to Prince Godric's private world of depravity and overindulgence. There were three doors to pick from in front of me. From behind the middle door, I heard muffled voices, so I hurried toward it and pressed my ear against it.

"Leave that thing alone. It's in a cage for a reason. It hisses and bites. I even saw smoke come out of its nose."

"I can't. It's so disgusting but also fascinating. It's got a weird leathery head."

That second voice was Prince Godric, and although I'd only heard Prince Jasper speak a few times, I was almost certain that was him in the room, too. But, most importantly, the thing they were talking about sounded like Hodgepodge. He was alive!

"I'm tired, brother. You've had me up all night talking nonsense. It's dawn, and I need to sleep," Prince Jasper said. "If all you wanted me here for was to show off and taunt that beast, this has been a waste of my time."

"This isn't nonsense. Our futures rest on this success."

"You mean, our future rests on my shoulders and getting that sullen-faced hag pregnant as soon as possible," Prince Jasper said.

Prince Godric laughed. "I can always help if you're having trouble. She's not so bad to look at."

"She whines, cries, and complains all the time. I have to force her to smile when we're in public. Why would I want to go anywhere near her?"

"Think of the blessed child that'll be born into this world when you have a successful union." Prince Godric's chuckle was laced with icy abrasiveness.

"You're lucky it's not you. You got out of this because you're the younger child. It makes me sick."

"What it means, dearest older brother, is you automatically inherit everything. I get nothing."

"I've already said I'll share power when the time comes."

"And I believe every word that comes out of your mouth. We've been raised by the same ruthless monsters, so I know how your mind works."

Something metallic rattled, and I fisted my hands. It sounded like cage bars being struck.

"I thought I knew how your mind worked, but this plan will end in disaster. People won't stand for it," Prince Jasper said.

There was a familiar hiss, and it took all my restraint not to fling myself into the room to protect Hodgepodge.

"You're talking about the peasants. They're pointless and powerless," Prince Godric said.

"Those peasants are asking questions about why people are going missing," Prince Jasper said. "I've been on the streets doing Mother's enforced meet-and-greet, and they're whispering. You're not being careful. You said you'd only pick the women that didn't matter."

"Everyone I picked was worthless. And everyone else will understand that sacrifices must be made to restore order."

"They won't be so understanding when they realize we caused the disorder in the first place."

"Keep your dumb mouth shut and they'll never know." The bars of a cage rattled again. "Maybe your fiancée would like this creature as a pet. She could parade it around on a leash or have it turned into a pair of shoes when she tires of it."

"Leave it alone and let me rest," Prince Jasper said. "Please, I'm exhausted. We've been going around in circles for hours, and we're never going to agree. You can keep me sleep-deprived for days, but I can't see the logic in chasing an ancient myth written by a wizard high off his gourd on magic mushrooms and angel dust."

"Don't back out now. You know this has to happen. We're doing the right thing. And if you want any hope of siring an heir, you'll support my plan or face our mother's fury."

"I've always supported a different approach to dealing with the dragons," Prince Jasper said. "They should never have been killed."

"It's safe. Go in now, while you can."

I just about jumped out of my skin when the disembodied voice whispered close to my ear. I looked around, but there was no one there. The strange voice had gotten me this far without getting caught, so I had to trust it.

I pushed open the door and edged inside. I was in another smaller room, and in front of me, there was a door standing open. I saw a glimpse of Prince Godric as he passed the door.

"Ruminating on the past gets us nowhere," he said. "It's happened, and we need a solution."

"I've read the book, but you don't even know if you're using the right sacrifice. You're stumbling around in the dark," Prince Jasper said. "Maybe the blood the dragons need to spring back to life isn't even human. They could want animal sacrifices. Have you tried goat?"

"Everything before moving on to the peasants. Nothing works!"

"Because you have no clue what you're doing."

There was a thump and a yelp. "Say that again. I'm doing this to save all of us."

"You're doing it to take power and gain control." Prince Jasper sounded like he was being choked. "I've had enough."

I crawled into the room on my hands and knees and ducked behind a chair. I peeked over the top and spotted Prince Godric, his back to the door and his hands around his brother's throat.

"You're pathetic. I should be the one taking control." Prince Godric snarled. "I'm doing everything to make things right."

"It's funny how you always find a justification for murder when it suits your purposes," Prince Jasper wheezed out.

"And I find it funny how you simper and bow before Mother and her ridiculous demands. She set you up for failure. And she's done that because she wants me to take over."

"You'll have to kill her before you do."

"That's the plan."

There was silence, and I held my breath, although I wasn't surprised to hear Prince Godric's head was full of murder and power grabs. Nasty little creep.

"You wouldn't," Prince Jasper said. "You'd really kill her?"

Prince Godric dropped his hold on his brother and shoved him. "Stick around for long enough, and you'll see exactly what I'm capable of."

"Not more sacrifices, though?" Prince Jasper's breathing was labored. "You can't take more women and expect to get away with it."

"We just need the right one. And as for the ones we've already got, we're moving them. They're useless, but they know too much, so I can't risk keeping them here."

"Moving them where?"

It was a question I wanted answered, too.

Prince Godric strode closer to my hiding place, his hands clenched. "I've got a contact at the docks. I've sold the women, and they'll soon be on a ship going overseas. With luck, most of them won't make it. The few who do will be so relieved they've been given a new start that they'll never risk coming back and facing my wrath. The truth won't get out. And even if it does, the dragons will be back, so no one will care about a few worthless, lost women."

I scowled as I remained crouched. Prince Godric was a monster, and his brother wasn't much better. I wasn't letting this happen. I didn't know how I'd stop it, but I'd make sure those women weren't shoved onto a ship and ripped away from everything they knew.

But before I did that, I was getting Hodgepodge back.

Chapter 14

My legs were cramping from staying crouched while I listened to the princes' continual bickering, but I didn't dare move in case I made a sound and they discovered me. I'd managed a few peeks around the room and had spotted the top of the cage. That was my focus.

"Please, brother. No more plotting." Prince Jasper headed to the window. "The sun is almost up."

"What of it? We can go to bed any time we choose. Or are you keen to fall into the arms of your soon-to-be bride?" Prince Godric's tone was full of derision as he joined his brother at the window.

"You'll be next. You may think you have our mother wrapped around your little finger, but she'll pick you a bride."

"I'll take her and continue to sow my wild oats wherever I please. Mother doesn't control me."

"More fool you for thinking that." Prince Jasper dodged a punch to the arm.

"The old hag won't be a problem for much longer. When I bring back the dragons and bend them to my will, she'll have no choice but to curtsy to me. Then you'll know you've picked the right side."

"We're family. We're not supposed to have sides."

"Then you're living a lie." Prince Godric slapped his brother on the shoulder. "One more drink."

Prince Jasper feebly protested, but within moments, they were sipping brandy and had moved to the other side of the elaborately decorated room and were studying documents on a table, their backs to me.

"Go now." The strange disembodied voice was still in my ear, but I was jumping less every time I heard it. I stayed crouched as I inched closer to Hodgepodge, my mouth dry and my palms sweaty.

I kept inching forward, almost forgetting to breathe until I made myself lightheaded. I focused on the cage. That was all that mattered, getting Hodgepodge. There was a ragged blanket inside and a lump underneath it. That must be him.

I stopped for a second behind a high-backed chair, my leg muscles screaming at me to stand. I risked a look over the top. The brothers were still absorbed in whatever was on the table as they continued to sip brandy and talk softly.

The blanket inside the cage twitched, and Hodgepodge's head appeared. He blinked several times as if he couldn't believe it was me, and then his attention turned to the princes, and he showed his sharp teeth.

I pressed a finger to my lips, although I knew he wouldn't do anything foolish to reveal what was going on. Still in a crouch, I reached the cage and eased the door open. A hinge squeaked, and I froze, my gaze flashing to the princes, but they were focused on what they were looking at, and they paid us no attention.

The second the gap was large enough, Hodgepodge squeezed through and jumped onto my shoulder. His heavy weight had never felt more welcome as he curled his tail around my neck and pressed his head against my cheek.

I held a hand against his side, feeling for any injuries, but there were no wounds, blood, or bruises.

He gestured his head at the door, and I needed no further encouragement to get as far away from the princes as possible.

Remaining low, I scuttled back to the door and out, away from danger. I didn't stand for fear I'd groan the second I stretched my muscles, so I continued my crouched walk until I was in the main corridor. I silently closed the door and let out an enormous sigh of relief.

"You took a risk, lassie, coming for me," Hodgepodge said, still with his head pressed against my cheek, emitting a purr of contentment.

"I'll always come for you when you need me." I lifted him off and looked him over before kissing his head repeatedly.

"I'm fine. Quit your fussing. What about you?"

I settled him back around my neck then hurried along the corridor to the top of the stairs, remembering to grab my cleaning bucket as I passed it. "You won't believe the tale I have to tell. But not here. The castle is waking, and we can't be seen on the upper levels." I tiptoed with haste down the private staircase. When I reached the bottom, I froze. Warwick was striding toward me.

Hodgepodge hissed. "I'll scratch his eyes out. You run for it."

"No! Let's see what he does." My heart thrummed in my chest as I looked at Warwick and my gaze locked with his. He stared at me in silence for a second then gently shook his head and gestured for me to carry on.

I nodded my thanks and hurried toward the servants' staircase, only breathing properly again when I was concealed behind the door and a welcome gloomy light surrounded us.

"Warwick just helped us!" Hodgepodge said. "Why didn't he arrest us and drag us down to the dungeon?"

"I'll tell you everything. But after that unwanted adventure, we need tea and cake."

It was late evening, and after speed cleaning the chamber before the next round of visitors, I took a few moments to sit between Emberthorn's claws with Hodgepodge, a mug of precious hot cocoa in my hand and a small sugared pastry in a napkin Alice had given me when I'd stopped by the kitchen.

I'd told Hodgepodge everything about my experience in the dungeon, finding him gone, the trapped women, and how Warwick had helped me get out.

Hodgepodge was still grumbling about that last point. "I don't trust Warwick." He had barely left my side all day, and I'd been glad of his company, my heart racing every time my thoughts had returned to my time in the dungeon. I'd been so close to losing everything I loved.

"I'm worried what he'll do too, but you saw how he assisted us when we were fleeing from the upper floors."

"Warwick could change his mind. He's always been fiercely loyal to the family."

"He said the same to me, but now I'm not so sure. The way he talked made me think he was more loyal to the dragons than the family, and now the dragons are gone, he's conflicted," I said.

"The family gives him shelter, food, and pay. With the dragons dead, his loyalty should be with them. And if he tells them you were confined to the dungeon, this will be over."

"Which is why we need to act fast. We have to stop that ship from leaving with the women in it." I finished my last bite of pastry, feeding a few large crumbs to Hodgepodge.

"Where are we getting help from?"

"When we finish here, we're going back to see Elara."

"To teach her a lesson?"

"To find out why she deceived us." I stood as I headed to the servants' tunnel. It hurt my heart that she'd betrayed us. Elara had always been our friend. More than that. I loved her. "I can't believe she works for the family. I have to know there's still goodness in her."

"If there isn't?"

"Then perhaps it will be payback time." I glanced over my shoulder as visitors' voices drifted closer. "Let's get out of here, Hodgie."

After my shift finished in the castle, I headed to the portal tunnels. There was a tunnel a ten-minute walk from Elara's cottage, and I wasted no time activating it and stepping through. We arrived in the middle of the dense, chilly, damp forest, the full moon barely peeking through the leaves overhead.

Hodgepodge was wrapped around my neck, concealed under the heavy cloak I wore, the hood pulled high. I walked with purpose, as silently as possible, toward Elara's house. I was angry and saddened by what she'd done, and I had to know why. Despite Hodgepodge trying to talk me out of this visit repeatedly, I was heartbroken she'd behaved this way, and I needed answers.

There was a single light on in a downstairs room as we approached. I slowed as two figures passed the window. Elara rarely had visitors and never this late.

"It could be someone from the Ithric family," Hodgepodge whispered. "They may have realized you've escaped from the dungeon, so they could be looking for you."

"I'm not important enough for a member of the family to seek me out," I murmured. "Maybe a guard, but I see no horse, and they wouldn't have come by foot."

"They used the tunnels, same as us. We can still turn back. It's not too late."

The front door opened, and Elara peered into the gloom. "Who's out there? I encourage you to leave before you're unable to."

"I'm going nowhere." I stepped closer until she could see me.

Elara sucked in a breath, and her mouth dropped open. "Bell! How... What are you doing here?"

"After what you did, you must be surprised to see me." I pulled back my cloak. "Did you think I'd be dead? Or maybe drained of blood, so I was too weak to move."

Tears filled her eyes as she ducked her head. "I'm so sorry, child. I had no choice."

"Granny, who is it?" A tall, willowy woman with amber hair appeared behind Elara, a quizzical expression on her face. "Are these friends of yours?"

"Very dear friends. This is Bell Blackthorn and Hodgepodge." Elara beckoned us closer. "Please, come in and let me explain."

I didn't move. "How do I know you won't drug us again?"

Elara reached for her granddaughter's hand. "Because the family kept their promise and returned to me what they'd taken."

I stared at Elara's granddaughter. "The Ithric family took you?"

The young woman looked confused. "I'm uncertain. I'm uncertain about a lot of things. It's why we're up so late. I'm Esmeralda Soothling. The last thing I remember, I was having supper with Granny, went for a walk, and then... well, I don't know. It's all a blur. Now, I'm back. You're the reason I was returned?"

"Please, come inside, Bell," Elara said. "There's a lot I need to explain. To you and Esmeralda."

Hodgepodge grumbled, but I pressed a hand against his side and headed to the door. I welcomed the warmth from the open fire as we settled around the kitchen table, although I kept my cloak on in case we needed to make a quick escape.

"Ginger tea?" Elara asked.

I shook my head. "You won't be surprised if I refuse all offers of food and drink from you."

She lowered her chin. "I understand. I am so sorry."

"I don't understand," Esmeralda said. "What's going on?"

"Your grandmother drugged us and handed us over to the Ithric family," Hodgepodge said.

Esmeralda's eyes flashed wide. "We're no friend of the family. It's why Granny lives in the middle of nowhere, surrounded by magic she's not supposed to use. The family spread rumors she used dark spells and incited trouble for us. We're fortunate she wasn't imprisoned or worse."

"It's hardly the middle of nowhere." Elara gently patted Esmeralda's shoulder. "But I've had battles with the family, and they don't forget an enemy, no matter how quietly I live my life."

"Why did you do it?" I asked her. "I came to you for help."

Elara settled in a seat between me and Esmeralda, her hands in her lap and her shoulders hunched. "Esmeralda came to stay a few months ago. I don't know how they learned of her visit, but the family sent guards to take her when she walked in the woods."

Esmeralda shook her head. "I have no memory of that happening. I have huge blank spots in my thoughts."

"They used magic to erase your memory," Elara said. "They must have been watching the area. I'd grown complacent, thinking I was immune from harm out here. But when I had something they valued, they revealed themselves."

"How is Esmeralda of value to the Ithric family?" I asked.

"She comes from a long line of ancient witches," Elara said. "As much as the Ithric family hates the idea that any other lineage is more powerful than them, the Soothling

Witches know magic they can only dream about. And we always marry well to grow our powers."

"They took Esmeralda, thinking what?" I asked. "They'd force her to cast spells for them?"

"I believe so," Elara said. "Fortunately for Esmeralda, the power hasn't developed in her."

Esmeralda scowled, and a flush of color flooded her cheeks. "I'm a late bloomer."

"Be grateful you are," Elara said gently. "When the family learned Esmeralda couldn't be useful to them, they kept her anyway. They said I'd get her back when I'd passed on enough useful information."

Hodgepodge blew smoke from his nose. "You were spying for them?"

"My granddaughter's life was on the line." Elara lifted her chin. "You'd do the same for Bell if they captured her."

Hodgepodge grumbled some coarse words but didn't protest, simply wrapped his tail around my wrist.

"When I came to you asking questions, you thought you were onto something?" I asked. "You drugged me and gave me to the family to get your granddaughter back?"

"The Ithric family knows trouble is coming for them. They may pretend to pay no attention to the peasants, as they call them, but they're worried. People want the dragons back, and the rumors grow daily that the Ithric family had a hand in what happened. When you came to me talking about the stolen book, the missing women, and the blood sacrifices, I knew they'd see you as a troublemaker and want to silence you."

I looked at Esmeralda and then Elara. It hurt that she'd betrayed me, but I understood why. That knowledge barely lessened the ache in my chest or the sense of loss that would never be smoothed over.

"What did you do after you drugged me and Hodgepodge?" I asked.

"I took you to the dungeon, but I kept your head covered so no one saw you. I handed you to the guards, and they took you away." Elara's bottom lip trembled. "How did you get out? I haven't stopped thinking about you."

"I shouldn't tell you how I escaped. You may pass the information onto the family and attempt to destroy someone else's life."

A tear trickled down Elara's cheek. "If there'd been any other way, I'd have done it. And after I delivered you and left details of the information we'd discussed, they returned Esmeralda to me. I got what I wanted."

"By giving me up." I had to look away and take a breath. This betrayal hurt.

Hodgepodge laid his head against my chest and hummed softly to calm me.

"Who did you speak to from the family?" I asked. "I was left in the dungeon, but no one came to interrogate me."

"I sent them a note, but I don't know who read it. I didn't use your name. You must have gotten out just in time." Elara let out a sigh. "I'm glad."

I set my hands flat on the table. "Now I'm back, and you owe me."

"Granny, you must help Bell and Hodgepodge." Esmeralda clasped Elara's hand.

"Of course. Whatever they need. I can give you new identity papers and funds to send you on your way. You can't stay in the castle. It won't be safe."

"Maybe it's not safe, but the dragons are there, and I'm not abandoning them. And I'm not abandoning the women the Ithric family have taken," I said.

"You want to set them free?" Hope lit Elara's eyes.

"No one else does, so it's down to me and Hodgepodge to fix this mess," I said. "And I need all the help I can get. Magic. I need magic."

Esmeralda grinned. "Good for you. If I could cast spells, I'd join you. I hate that family for taking me and forcing Granny to do this to you."

"You're going nowhere near that castle ever again." Elara was already on her feet and sorting through a large wooden chest in the corner of the room. "You need to leave."

"I'm staying with you," Esmeralda said. "What if they come back?"

"If they come back, you'll be long gone." Elara lifted a small, blackened wooden flute. "This can conjure bad weather. Be careful not to play it too vigorously, or you'll wind up trapped inside a tornado."

"Could be useful," Hodgepodge said. "What else have you got? Make it good. Bell almost died. So did I. And I had to put up with Prince Godric the Gross prodding me in places no wyvern should be prodded."

"A potion of concealment. Three drops only or you'll remain invisible." Elara set the potion bottle on the side. "And this ring."

I leaned forward, excited by the prospect of using powerful magic. "What does the ring do?"

"Gives you strength. It's a ring of power. Wear that, and you could most likely defeat Warwick if you had to stand against him."

I held my tongue. Although Elara was helping, I no longer trusted her and wouldn't share who was a potential ally.

Elara gathered the items and set them all on the table in front of me. Then she pressed a kiss to my cheek. "And that's a kiss of dragon luck. You'll need it going up against the Ithric family."

"I'm doing the right thing, and that means I must win."

There was sadness in Elara's eyes as she acknowledged my comment. "Prince Godric thinks he's right, sacrificing women to get back the dragons. He needs the family line to continue, so he'll fight just as hard as you to win." She dropped to her knees and caught hold of my hand. "Please, forgive me. If there'd been any other way..."

I squeezed her hand. It still hurt, but she'd done it to help her family. "I do. And I appreciate the magic items."

"We should go," Hodgepodge said. "It'll be light soon, and we need to be back at the castle, faking business as usual."

I nodded, said goodbye to Esmeralda and Elara, and hurried away from the cottage, the magic items tucked in my skirt pockets.

"What do we do now?" Hodgepodge asked.

I drew in a deep breath. "Now, we get the team together and stop Prince Godric."

Chapter 15

I paced my room the next morning, my hands gripped together and Hodgepodge balanced on my shoulders. I wasn't sure everyone had received the messages I'd sent. It was a few hours before dawn, and I needed to know I had backup before continuing this quest.

There was a soft rap on my door, and I dashed to open it. Evander leaned on the doorjamb, a smile on his roguishly handsome face.

"You came." I stepped back to let him in and quietly closed the door.

"How could I resist such an offer? Bell Blackthorn and her scaled friend are going on a quest, and they need my assistance. I had to find out what you have planned. What quest is this? Are you expanding your cleaning empire and taking on a new wing in the castle?" Evander chuckled. "Or perhaps you hope to clean the west turret and encounter Mad Lord Crosby. Make a new friend, perhaps."

I thumped his arm. "Shush. This is serious. I'll wait for the others before I tell you everything."

"Others? You need more than me to complete your daring quest?" Evander arched an eyebrow as he dropped into the only comfortable chair in the room.

"For what I have planned, I definitely do."

A moment later, Astrid arrived. She strode in, looking healthy and not like she'd recently been stabbed, and grinned at me.

"Thanks for coming at such short notice," I said.

"I owe you. You patched me up after my last misadventure." Her eyes narrowed as she realized we weren't alone. "What's he doing here?"

"It's always a pleasure to see you too, Astrid." Evander sat back, his legs splayed as he smiled at her. "Gotten yourself tangled in more trouble, recently?"

"Mind your business." She glared at me. "You can't trust him."

"I have no choice," I said. "And Evander has always helped me when I've needed it."

"He'll trade with the devil if the deal is good enough," Astrid said.

"Maybe we need someone like that on the team."

"Team!" Astrid backed toward the door. "No, I work alone. It's safer that way."

I grabbed her arm as she turned to go. "Hey! You do owe me. Sure, I patched you up after you got in trouble, but you lied to me."

Astrid glared at my hand, but I held on. "I did? When was that?"

"She tells so many lies, she can't remember which one she told you." Evander laughed when Astrid bared her teeth at him in a savage smile.

"The book!" I had the stolen book on the table. "You said you were taking me to the castle to see it. You failed to mention you were also planning on stealing gold and jewels from the family."

She looked embarrassed for half a second before her confident demeanor reappeared. "Oh! That. That was nothing. A simple case of multitasking. I needed resources, and so did you."

"Or you took me into the castle as a decoy. You hoped the guards would hear me and be distracted so they wouldn't notice you slipping into the family rooms to steal from them." I set my hands on my hips. "I got questioned by Warwick and Prince Godric."

Astrid pressed a hand against her heart. "As if I'd do such a thing."

"As if you wouldn't," Evander said, looking like he was thoroughly enjoying the show. "You'd sell out your own sister to avoid being arrested."

"Like you wouldn't."

"This team doesn't have to be permanent," I said to her. "But I need backup for what I'm about to do. Astrid, you're stealthy and sneaky. You know your way around places I don't. And you have good connections. I need us to work together one time, and then we're even. I'll never ask you for anything ever again."

Astrid rolled her eyes. "Sure, sure. Enough with the flattery. Just this once."

"We know you're a lone ranger." Evander smirked and sank down in the chair, looking like he was ready for sleep.

A second later, there was another knock on the door. I walked over and opened it. Warwick stood outside, his expression grim.

"I didn't think you'd come," I said softly.

"Until five minutes ago, neither did I." He brushed past me and into the room.

Evander jumped to his feet, and Astrid drew a long, thin blade from its sheath on her hip. I threw myself between them and held my hands out, Hodgepodge hissing fiercely, the ruff around his neck fully extended.

"Why did you bring a member of the royal guard here?" Astrid spat out. "Is this a trap?"

"No! No trap."

"Bell, have you lost your mind?" Evander was in a crouch, his hands tightly fisted.

"Warwick has been helping me," I said. "Give me a minute to explain, and—"

"There's no way I'm working with Warwick. Or him!" Astrid inclined her head at Evander. "Evander's a reckless idiot, but Warwick would slit my throat in my sleep if Prince Godric told him to. He can't think for himself."

Warwick flashed her a fierce grin. "You don't know me if that's what you believe."

Astrid's top lip curled. "How have you gotten Bell on your side? What have you got on her?"

"Nothing! Listen to me. I got in trouble after I trusted someone I shouldn't. I ended up in the castle dungeon. Prince Godric almost saw me, but Warwick got me out. He saved me from the cell. He set me free." My gaze shot between the trio, waiting to see if any of them would make a move.

Neither Evander nor Astrid spoke. Both appeared surprised.

"It's true! Warwick's having doubts about working for the family. He knows what they're doing, and he wants it to stop, don't you?" I turned to Warwick, whose gaze blazed as he glared at the others.

He slowly removed his hand from the hilt of his sword and nodded. "I've had a lot of thinking to do recently. Finding Bell in a cell was the final straw. I've worked here as long as Bell, and in that time, I've only ever seen her do good deeds. And her devotion to the dragons is beyond reproach."

"Don't tell me you're soft on Bell?" Evander smirked. "She's way out of your league."

"Stop that. It has nothing to do with it," I said. "This is about the dragons and stopping the family from doing the wrong thing to bring them back."

"You don't want the dragons back?" There was a note of caution in Astrid's words.

"Of course. But there must be another way. Prince Godric stealing women and keeping them locked in the dungeon is wrong."

"You still can't trust Warwick," Evander said.

"He's done nothing but help me," I said. "I have to believe he'll continue to do so."

"Then you're a fool." Astrid stepped back and sheathed her blade.

Warwick relaxed a fraction. "I've been questioning the family's methods for some time, and when Prince Godric announced he wanted to expand his plans, I couldn't agree with him."

"Plans to do what?" Evander asked.

Before Warwick could answer, there was another knock on the door. I opened it. Griffin stood outside. "Hey. What's up? I came as soon as I could."

"Thanks. You're the last one to arrive. Come in."

Griffin stepped in and froze when he saw everyone else. "What's going on?"

I shut the door and leaned against it. "You all know each other for one reason or other, so I don't need to make the introductions."

"I know Astrid. I've almost arrested her a dozen times," Warwick said.

"Me too," Evander said smugly. "But I always get away from you."

"I have a long list of crimes you've both committed," Warwick muttered. "You'll get what's coming to you."

"Not now they won't," I said. "We leave the past where it is, and we focus on what's going on now. You all know my concerns. I've asked you to help solve this problem, and so far, you've all been supportive."

"That doesn't mean we'll continue to be," Astrid said. "And I don't work for free."

"I'm not expecting you to. But you owe me, Astrid. And Warwick, you're unhappy about what the Ithric family is doing, and you want it to stop."

He nodded.

I looked at Evander. "I can pay you. Not right away, but if you help, I'll not only owe you a favor, but I'll reward you."

"That's a tempting offer." Evander rocked back on his heels. "What could I possibly want from you?"

"Don't push your luck," Warwick growled.

Evander laughed. "I love a quest. That's my payment. I'm intrigued as to what you have planned."

I narrowed my eyes at him then turned to Griffin. "I hope our friendship means you want to help. Of course, I'll understand if you aren't available. This won't be easy."

"How is a one-armed former fighter reduced to cleaning the drains any good to you?" Evander asked.

Griffin lunged at him, a small blade in his hand.

"Are you out of your tiny minds?" Astrid snapped. "This room barely has enough space to swing a sword. Start a fight, and we'll all get hurt."

Evander dodged away from Griffin, a smirk on his face. "Still sore about losing to me?"

"I didn't lose! I didn't want her, anyway."

"Who are they arguing over?" I stood by Astrid as the men eye-balled each other.

"Some girl. Griffin asked her out then Evander stole her off him before they had their first date."

Evander lifted a hand, magic swirling around his fingers. "You can't steal what doesn't belong to you. She simply made the better choice."

Griffin's eyes narrowed, and his grip tightened on the hilt of his blade. "You talk too much, Evander. Let me see what I can do to change that." Without warning, he lunged forward, moving with surprising agility. His blade sliced through the air, aimed straight for Evander's chest. He deftly sidestepped, the blade missing him by a hair's breadth.

Evander retaliated by unleashing a burst of magical energy. Arcane tendrils shot from his fingertips, aiming to ensnare Griffin. He ducked and rolled, evading the attack, his movements fluid and precise.

"You're fast," Evander admitted, a grin playing on his lips. "Let's see if you can keep up with this." He channeled magic into his feet and darted forward, moving so quickly it was almost as if he'd translocated, and launched a flurry of blows, each punch accompanied by a burst of magical energy. Griffin parried most of them with his blade, but a few landed on his chest, causing him to stagger back.

I stepped forward to stop them, but Astrid grabbed my arm.

"Let them duke this one out. They've been niggling at each other for months. They get this out of their system and they can focus on your quest."

I wasn't sure my room could withstand too many magical blasts and blades swings, but with Astrid and Hodgepodge encouraging me to stay back, I had no choice but to watch.

Gritting his teeth, Griffin swung his blade in a wide arc. Evander barely had time to react, bringing up a protective shield of magic to deflect the blade. The force of the blow sent him skidding across the small room and thumping into my bed.

"You're not the only one with tricks," Griffin grunted, sweat beading on his forehead.

Evander gathered magic into a concentrated ball of fire. He was no longer smiling as he ran at Griffin.

"Stop! Enough. This is my home, and you don't get to burn it to the ground." I tried to push between them, but they were too close together, fiery magic sparking around them. I grabbed the ring of power from the table, slipped it on one finger, clutched the back of Evander's shirt, and threw him across the room.

Everyone stared open-mouthed as Evander hit the wall and slid down it with a groan.

"What the heck was that?" he asked.

"One of our advantages." I held up my hand and showed them the ring. "But we must work together or this all falls apart."

"You've got my attention." Evander stood and dusted down his clothing. "Nice move, Bell. I didn't see it coming."

"When I was in Prince Godric's chambers..." I started, but Astrid interrupted.

"Wait, why were you insane enough to go in there?"

"You went in when you stole from him. Why shouldn't I?"

She arched an eyebrow. "Fair point. What did you take?"

"He had Hodgepodge. I got him back," I said. "That's beside the point. When I was in there, he was talking to his brother. The women they've taken are being moved. Prince Godric is concerned they know too much, so he sold them, and they're to be put on a ship that is leaving soon. I need to find out what ship and how we can prevent it from leaving. We're setting those women free."

"You've got my support. Besides, I have a score to settle with Prince Godric." Griffin looked down at where his arm had once been.

"I can't continue to support the Ithric family," Warwick said. "Since the dragons have gone, their methods and motives have become twisted."

"They were twisted before the dragons were killed," Evander said.

Warwick nodded. "They've grown even darker. I stand with you, Bell."

Evander inclined his head. "Like I said, I love a challenge, and this sounds fun. Some of those women will be grateful I rescue them and offer me a special thank you."

Astrid shoved him in the shoulder. "Keep your hands off. I'm coming along to ensure none of these morons screw up and end up stuck on a ship on the other side of the ocean."

Evander chuckled. "What can I do about it if they find me an irresistible hero?"

I pursed my lips. "Behave. Those women will be vulnerable."

Warwick stepped forward. "We'll help, but this quest could get us killed. We're not playing a game. The Ithric family comes down hard on anyone who goes up against them. If you do this, it'll change everything."

I looked at the magic items Elara had given me and then at the group. I placed a hand against Hodgepodge's side and gathered strength from his solid form. "I understand. But we can't let them get away with this."

"Go big or go home." Evander clapped his hands together.

"Such an idiot," Astrid said. She smiled at me. "But he's kind of right. How do you want to do this?"

Chapter 16

My eyes burned with exhaustion, but I kept up the pretense of being my normal bright and breezy self as I walked around the stone chamber with Hodgepodge, clearing up spilled offerings of wine and food and collecting the debris the visitors had left behind.

I wasn't just cleaning, though. I was on a mission. So was everyone else who'd agreed to get involved in what was most likely a suicide mission. Griffin was in the yard, hanging around with the gate guards to see if he could hear news about the impending departure of the ship and when the women would be moved.

Warwick, as usual, was with Prince Godric, with a plan to stay close and listen to his conversations. And, if the opportunity arose, he'd look through Prince Godric's papers and see if there were clues relating to the ship.

Evander had been dispatched to the docks and was stealthily checking ship departures and any signs of suitable ships making ready to depart. He had a wide network of connections, so it wouldn't seem unusual he was asking around. If any questions were raised, he planned to tell them he was considering a move abroad and was looking for a suitable passage.

Astrid breezed through the chamber doorway, confidence in her stride as she walked toward me.

"How did you get past the guards?" I asked. "The chamber doesn't open to visitors for another five minutes."

She rubbed her fingers together in the universal sign of money. "The family's guards aren't as well-trained as they think they are. They'll turn their heads the other way for the right incentive."

"Are you sure you want to do this?" Astrid had been given the most dangerous task. She was breaking into Prince Godric's private chambers.

"I couldn't think of a better way to start my day." She grinned at me. "Relax. It won't be the first time I've been there. Our charming prince is always leaving goodies around to be taken by those who are more deserving."

"How many times have you stolen from Prince Godric?"

"I've lost count. And why not? He steals the joy out of everyone else's life, so it's a small price for him to pay."

"Take this. It'll help you get inside." I pulled the potion of concealment from a skirt pocket.

She waved away my offer. "I don't need your magic. I've been doing this since I was six years old. My mother used to take me with her when she needed someone to crawl through small spaces and open doors. I was practically born into this lifestyle."

"I'll feel better if you use it."

"You keep it. It may come in handy."

I reluctantly tucked the potion back into my underskirt. "Any news from the others?"

"Evander's checked in once. Nothing strange going on at the docks. Some of the ships are loading, ready to depart, but they're cargo ships, and the captains have confirmed they aren't taking foot passengers."

"They could be lying. Or they've been bribed to remain silent about their secret cargo."

"Evander is a better briber and more persuasive. Besides, he knows his people. His father owned the Green Empress. He's been among sailors ever since he was a toddler."

"He never told me that."

Astrid shrugged. "He doesn't talk about his past much. Too many demons lurking. Seen anything while you've been cleaning these beauties?" She patted Emberthorn's broad snout.

"Nothing. I've stayed inside the tunnels and watched the visitors. So far, it's a typical day."

"It's far from that. If this works, things will never be the same for the Ithric family."

"So long as we get those women free and out of the dungeon," I said.

Astrid narrowed her gaze. "You don't think they'll replace them with more, do you?"

"Not once people know what's going on. They may think we're powerless peasants, but if we all stand up against them, it'll work."

"I love your optimism. I used to be like that." Astrid looked over her shoulder as a gaggle of voices approached the main entrance. "That's my cue to leave.

I'm off to see if princey boy is awake." She slipped into the servants' tunnels.

I followed her a few seconds later, concealing myself and leaning against the wall, Hodgepodge curled around my neck as we watched the visitors amble into the stone chamber, their offerings clasped in their hands.

Their gazes usually went first to the enormous height of the ceiling with its vast lead-lined glass roof then to the dragons. They all carried offerings, mostly food or drink, but there were also a few coins. They had to walk a designated route around each dragon, starting at the snout then moving in a clockwise direction until they returned to their start point.

Emberthorn was the first dragon visited, and he got most of the offerings, even though he'd jointly ruled with his brother. Emberthorn was a charismatic dragon, charming everyone with his benevolence and fair mind. Stormwing had been rougher but just as effective as a joint ruler.

"Ach. That little kiddie just spilled her drink all over Emberthorn's claws." Hodgepodge hissed softly. "It's bright red."

"The stain will come out. And if the real Emberthorn was standing there, he'd laugh about it. He always loved children."

"Not so much anymore. The dragon's curse put an end to children."

"Allegedly," I whispered.

"There are too many secrets in this place," Hodgepodge muttered. "We should have stayed safe by our cozy fireside and ignored this. Secrets bring trouble."

"Not for much longer."

"I'm not convinced anything will change. If there's an uprising and the family gets kicked out, will their replacement be any better?"

"We have to hope. Previous rulers weren't so bad," I murmured, focusing on the visitors as they circled the dragons and oohed and aahed about how magnificent they were. I hadn't thought ahead about what would happen when the truth came out. The Ithric family would be furious, and they'd want revenge. If they realized I was behind this stir of trouble, they'd come for me and Hodgepodge. We may have to flee the realm.

Despite the danger that lurked here, I didn't want that. This was the only home I knew.

I ate a small snack of almonds and fed Hodgepodge dried apple while we waited for the visitors to complete their route around the dragons and then slowly exit. When the last visitor had gone, that was our cue to go back in.

"Messy lot," Hodgepodge grumbled. "The offerings are fine, but why do they have to leave their empty food wrappers and dirt behind?"

"If they didn't, we wouldn't have a job." I looked at the dragons. "Did you enjoy your offerings? You got a wonderfully painted claw, Emberthorn." The drink the child spilled on him had seeped into the stone and stained it dark.

I used a tray to collect the offerings and set them to one side then briskly collected the dropped wrappers and tissues and swept the dirt.

I knelt to scrub Emberthorn's stained claw. "We're doing the right thing, aren't we? I know you can't answer me, but I'd like to think you approve. We're going against the Ithric family to make things better, not worse."

Hodgepodge hopped onto Emberthorn's snout and flopped onto his belly. "He agrees with you."

"How would you know that?"

"I'm part dragon. We have an affinity with each other."

"It's the first I'm hearing about it." Hodgepodge was a unique companion, his background a mystery and his parentage just as opaque. We'd connected at low moments in each other's lives. He'd been sick and hiding in a rotten tree stump, and my father had just walked away, claiming he could no longer deal with my mother's eccentricities.

I'd run to the woods to escape and cry, and we'd met when he'd slid out of his hiding place and licked the tears off my cheeks. The connection was instant, and I adored my curious scaled friend. We were rarely apart, and when I didn't have Hodgie by my side, it felt like a part of me was missing.

I finished my scrubbing, then slid around the side of the dragon. "It's freaky that Emberthorn's bones are inside here. The family entombed them."

"Which means they knew how and where he died," Hodgepodge said. "They collected the body because they killed him."

I shuddered at the thought of such cruelty. "If we get the dragons back, everything will be different."

"Things were certainly better before they disappeared." Hodgepodge stood and hopped onto Emberthorn's back. He paused and cocked his head. "He feels warm."

I pressed a hand against Emberthorn's side. He did feel warm. The sun sometimes heated the stones in the middle of the day, but this was the first public viewing session, so it was still rising and had yet to peek through the glass.

"I want everyone in full military uniform for the chancellor's visit. No exceptions. I'll even wear my damned uniform, so he doesn't think he can speak over me again."

I froze. I recognized Prince Godric's voice, and it sounded worryingly close.

"Of course. Some of the men are on patrol. You sent them to the eastern quadrant to quell the unrest." Warwick's reassuringly calm voice was also in the mix.

"Recall them. I don't want him thinking our numbers are down. Tell them to deal with the troublemakers in the swiftest fashion. No messing around with trials or evidence." Prince Godric's footsteps echoed around the stone chamber as he entered. His attention was on Warwick, who walked beside him, and he didn't see the bucket of water in his path. Before I could cry out a warning, his foot slammed into it, knocking it over and sending dirty water spilling across the floor.

Prince Godric slipped and skidded forward. Had it not been for Warwick's fast thinking, he would have landed on his butt, but Warwick grabbed him under the arms and hauled him to his feet.

"What the hell is going on in here?" Prince Godric shoved Warwick away and glared around the room. "What lunatic just tried to kill me?"

I grabbed Hodgepodge and concealed him behind Emberthorn. "Not a word. Stay here."

"If you don't come out this second, I'll have you thrashed to within an inch of your life," Prince Godric said. "Who assaulted me?"

"If I may, sir, you kicked the bucket of water," Warwick said.

"I didn't ask for your opinion."

Despite every nerve in my body telling me to remain hidden and silent, I stepped out and curtsied. "My apologies, Your Royal Highness. I didn't think anyone would be passing through the stone chamber while it was closed. I was cleaning."

"You! Again! Why am I always running into you?"

"I spend most of my life in here. It's important to make the chamber nice for visitors." I remained in my curtsied position, my head down.

"Stand. Look at me."

I slowly raised myself to my full height and met his gaze for a second. Those cold eyes made me queasy.

Prince Godric strode over. He placed a finger under my chin and lifted it higher, so I had no choice but to look at him. "Why are you here?"

"I... I've worked for the family since I was seventeen. This is my job."

"Always with the dragons?"

"No, general cleaning at first, but then the position became available, and I was offered it."

A spark of something I didn't like lit Prince Godric's gaze. "I remember, now. Your mother used to clean the stone chamber. What happened to her?"

I remained silent.

His brow arched. "Forget your own mother? Warwick, what was she to the castle?"

"I believe Bell's mother worked diligently for the family as a chambermaid."

"Why haven't I seen her around if she's such an upstanding member of staff?"

"She died," I whispered.

"Not sacked because she got old and slow?" Prince Godric circled me slowly, giving me a full view of Warwick. Although his expression was blank, a muscle in his jaw twitched. "You're married?"

"No."

"Children?"

"I'm childfree."

"What about family?"

"It's just me."

"All alone in this world." Prince Godric brushed a hand against my shoulder. "Unless you count your curious friendship with the dragons."

"I worship the dragons just like everybody else," I replied.

He sniffed. "Come to my chamber tonight. I have things that require cleaning."

I gulped and took a step back. "My job is here. I'm not permitted into the family's chambers."

"I've given you permission. Nine o'clock."

I shook my head. "I work here until midnight."

His eyes narrowed. "Are you disobeying me?"

"No! But I must be here."

"The dragons won't miss you while you're... assisting me."

"I should ask—" Prince Godric's hand hit my cheek so hard I didn't see it coming. I spun around, stars in my vision and tears filling my eyes as warm wetness leaked from my cut lip. I landed on Emberthorn, my hands splayed, my face pressed against his snout.

"Know your place, or you'll end up in the dungeon," Prince Godric snarled. "There's nothing I despise more than a disobedient woman. You should be grateful I'm showing you attention. You're hardly in your prime years."

I stayed where I was, too stunned to move and not wanting to face Prince Godric because he'd see my tears. They weren't shed because I was sad. They were partly due to shock, but they mainly leaked out of my eyes because I was angry and humiliated.

"Stay here amongst the dirt and the drudge. You're not worth my time. Warwick, with me." Prince Godric marched away, and a few seconds later, Warwick followed him.

Hodgepodge appeared by my foot and stared up at me, a hissing snarl rumbling out of him. I shook my head. I didn't want Hodgepodge to be heard and captured again.

I didn't move until the stone chamber had fallen silent, and a glance over my shoulder showed we were alone. I gathered Hodgepodge into a cuddle and sat between Emberthorn's claws, feeling safe with my wyvern and my dragon.

"I'll destroy him," Hodgepodge said. "Vicious, nasty little coward. He wouldn't dare do that to someone he considered an equal."

I swiped away a stray tear. "I've heard rumors he goes after the serving women."

"And now he's noticed you," Hodgepodge said. "He'll keep coming until he gets what he wants."

I kissed Hodgepodge's head, my stomach churning with fear. What we were doing was too hard. I'd gotten caught up in the excitement of a quest, thinking I could help those who needed rescuing. But now, I was the one who needed rescuing from Prince Godric and his slimy clutches. The thought of him touching me made my spine clench.

"You were right, Hodgepodge. We should have stayed quiet and out of the way. Then we would have been safe like we always were. Prince Godric would never have noticed me."

Hodgepodge rested his head on my chest and looked up at me. "We were never safe, lassie. We were just hiding from a horrible truth. Reality would have bitten us, eventually."

I waved a hand in front of my face. Prince Godric must have hit me harder than I'd realized because my vision was hazy. I reached into a pocket and pulled out a handkerchief, dabbing at my eyes and nose. When I removed it, there was a smear of blood on the white cloth.

I stood on shaky knees, holding Hodgepodge against my chest. "I need a tonic. My head is throbbing, and I can't afford to get sick."

Hodgepodge tensed and slid up to my shoulder. He made a noise I'd never heard from him before. A throaty grumble-growl. "Bell, you need to see this."

"I need to mop up that water, and then we have to get out before the visitors arrive." I took a step toward the bucket, but Hodgepodge's fierce hiss had me stopping. "What's wrong?"

"Turn around. Look at Emberthorn."

I pivoted on my heel to discover a smear of my blood on Emberthorn's snout. But it wasn't that catching my attention. It was the smoke drifting from his giant stone nostrils.

Chapter 17

I stumbled away from the smoking dragon until my feet hit the fallen bucket, and I almost slipped on the damp floor. It couldn't be. After all these years of hoping the dragons would come back, Emberthorn was finally stirring.

I shook my head then blinked several times. He returned my uncalm blinks with one blink of his own.

"It must be because of your blood," Hodgepodge whispered. "You woke him."

I lifted my fingers and touched the warm dampness on my cheek. One of Prince Godric's rings had struck me when he slapped my face. "My blood isn't powerful, though. It would take a master magic user to wake the dragons."

"Not according to the book." Hodgepodge had his tail curled so tightly around my neck I had to pry a finger underneath it so I could breathe properly. "Remember what it said. There was nothing about power or complicated spells. It was about goodness and a pure heart."

"There's nothing special about me." I was unable to turn my gaze from Emberthorn. He was still made of stone, but he looked alive. The stone gently pulsed, suggesting it could shatter at any moment. "Hodgepodge, what do we do?"

"You free me," the words whispered around us.

"Did you hear that?" I asked Hodgepodge.

Hodgepodge's head whipped around. "There's no one else in here."

"It's not the first time I've heard that voice. When I came to rescue you from Prince Godric's chambers, it guided me, making sure I got in and out without being seen." I took a tentative step toward Emberthorn. "Was that you? Have you been helping me all this time?"

Smoke billowed from the dragon's nostrils. "Bell Blackthorn, I was too weak to do anything but lay here and submit to the whims of the family, but then you appeared. You came every day with words of kindness and your songs. At first, they sustained me. Then my strength grew."

My mouth hung open, a torrent of emotions pouring through me and hitching my pulse. "Your visitors must help, too. And the offerings they bring show how much they miss you."

"We only needed one offering. Although we appreciate the gifts and are happy to know people still desire us to rule, you were the one we've been waiting for."

I looked at Stormwing. "He's awake, too?"

"Sadly, my brother was badly treated. His fiery nature meant he resisted and killed several of his assailants. Although, I'll confess to biting off a head or two when cornered. They punished him. Broke his bones into many pieces. I sense him, but it'll take a long time for him to heal. He may never be his old self."

I stepped closer and rested a shaking hand on Emberthorn's snout. The stone vibrated under my touch. It felt hot.

"Bell can't be put in danger," Hodgepodge said. "If she helps you, you must look after her."

"That's a given. We always look after the Dracarys Emissary," Emberthorn said.

"She's in the book!" I said. "The Dracarys Emissary is your connection to other magic users."

"In a way. Previous emissaries have acted as a liaison between the dragons and other magic rulers who desire a say in running the realm."

"You didn't have a liaison for the Ithric family," I said.

"They forbade it. They wanted us to work directly with them. Of course, we were cautious, but we wanted the best for the realm."

"You didn't get it," Hodgepodge said. "The Ithric family did this to you, didn't they?"

Emberthorn growled. "They did. And for that, they must pay. But I can do nothing while I am stuck like this. I may have been awakened, but I'm far from free. There is complicated magic binding us to this place."

I looked over my shoulder. There was barely any time left before the visitors came in. "Hodgepodge, I need you to cause a distraction."

He tensed. "I could run past the guards. Nip a few ankles."

"You'll be able to do much more than that if you're invisible." I pulled out the potion of concealment. "Give the visitors a fright and make them think the castle is haunted. That should cause confusion and slow things down. Don't get trodden on, though."

He readily opened his mouth and accepted three drops of the potion. A few seconds later, he shuddered and disappeared. I felt his snout press against my cheek, and then he was gone. Less than thirty seconds later, there were screams from the corridor as the guards yelled and something smashed.

"You have a worthy companion," Emberthorn said. "A dragon in miniature form. He is unique."

"Hodgepodge is the best. I'd never be without him." I took a few deep breaths, simply staring at Emberthorn. The dragons were back. They were really back, and it was because of my blood.

"Don't doubt yourself, Bell," he said. "You're kind, loyal, and true to those you serve. And that includes us. We would have no hope if it weren't for you."

"You're sure you've got the right person?" I said.

"The family you were born into, the status you hold in society, the way you look, even the accent you have is meaningless. It is how you behave, your actions toward yourself and others that reveal your true nature. You have never said a cruel word to anyone. And many have deserved it."

"I've thought plenty of them."

"None of us are perfect. But you act with integrity, and the care you've taken of me and my brother will stay with us forever. As I hope you'll stay with us, too."

"I have no plans to go anywhere. Although, if the Ithric family finds out what I'm attempting, I may have no choice, unless I plan on spending the rest of my days in their dungeon."

"I've been listening to your plans to save the women. Again, another example of your goodness."

"I can't turn my back on them," I said. "And I want to help you, too. What can I do to free you from the stone? You're not in any pain, are you?"

"No pain. Magic reduced us to this, but it also keeps us suspended in this form. Fortunately, the Ithric family weren't clever in their attempts to destroy us. By encasing our bones within these statues, they gave us an opportunity to return. But we need the words of release."

"Someone's coming!" Hodgepodge's invisible form thumped into my leg. "It's Lady Isolda and her assistants."

"They're coming in here?" I raced over and grabbed the fallen bucket before wiping a large rag over the floor to remove the dampness. If anything looked out of place, Lady Isolda would be suspicious and start paying attention to the dragons.

"We can't let them see Emberthorn smoking! Hurry. Hide the smoke." Hodgepodge thumped across the floor. "Hold your breath, dragon. They can't know you're awake or they'll smash you into a thousand pieces."

I grabbed my largest cleaning cloth and threw it over Emberthorn's head. "Don't move."

Emberthorn grew silent, with just the faintest puff of smoke drifting out from under the cloth. I pinned the corner then grabbed a large scrubbing brush and set to work on removing my blood from his snout.

Lady Isolda's fast, high-heeled footsteps entered the stone chamber. Her assistant's hurried footsteps matched hers as they dashed along to keep up with her.

"I want my sons in my chambers in ten minutes," she said.

"They're out," one of her trembling assistants said. "Prince Godric left a moment ago with Warwick. And Prince Jasper had breakfast early before leaving."

"I didn't ask for details of their movements. I want them back here."

"Of course. I'll send word they need to return."

"What's the delay?" Lady Isolda's voice rang out across the chamber.

I kept my back turned, scrubbing the stone, pretending I didn't know she was talking to me.

"You! With the scrubbing brush. Why are the visitors not here presenting their offerings? We have three barons visiting today, and they always leave generous donations."

I turned and curtsied. "Lady Isolda. I... I don't know."

She marched over. "The guards weren't on the door, and the visitors have scattered. Several of them were yelling about a ghost biting them. Superstitious nonsense."

I kept my gaze lowered. "I know nothing about that."

"And what's wrong with the dragon? Why is he covered?"

"A drink was spilled on him. I'm using a deep cleaning paste of baking soda and vinegar to remove the stain. It's a wonderful solution that removes marks from almost anything."

She waved a hand in the air dismissively. "Spare me your tedious knowledge. Get him uncovered before the visitors enter."

"He'll be ready in less than a minute," I replied with another curtsy.

She pursed her lips then turned and strode out of the stone chamber.

I stopped scrubbing and dropped my brush, leaning my head against Emberthorn's snout. I jerked back. "Sorry. That was disrespectful. All the times I've leaned against you or sat between your claws when I drank my hot chocolate and complained."

"Your company has always been welcome. And I was glad I could provide you shelter when you needed it," Emberthorn said. "You have nothing to apologize for."

"I have one thing," I said. "I know you think highly of this Dracarys Emissary idea, but I'm not powerful enough to free you and your brother. You've made a mistake. It isn't me."

"Ignore Bell. She always underestimates herself," Hodgepodge said. "She's the best person I know. I like few people, but I'd do anything for her."

"We're aware of her self-deprecation. And as charming as it is, things must change," Emberthorn said. "You need to believe in yourself, Bell, or this mission will fail."

I appreciated his faith in me, but my spells were basic and revolved around cleaning. I could manage a light ball when necessary, but that was about it.

"You have everything you need inside you," Emberthorn said.

I tilted my head. "Did you read my mind?"

"Your emotions."

I narrowed my eyes. "I don't. But hold tight. I know someone who can help us."

Hodgepodge shuddered on my shoulder, popping back into view. He shook himself from snout to tail. "That was fun. I bit five ankles. Where are we going?"

"To see Seraphina. She knows everything about dragons. She can help us figure out how to release them." I grabbed my cleaning equipment. "Emberthorn, stay silent and play at being a stone dragon while the visitors come in. Can you do that?"

"I've been doing it for years, so it'll be no hardship. And I enjoy seeing the visitors, even the children who spill their sweet drinks on me."

"I'll be back as quickly as I can." I tucked my cleaning equipment into the tunnel then dashed through the corridors to Seraphina's study. She'd spent her life researching dragons and knew all about their customs, laws, and behavior. She'd know if it was possible to bring them back to their full glory, now they'd stirred to life.

I blew out a steadying breath. Because of my blood, the dragons had returned. How was that possible?

I knocked on her study door, but no one answered. I tried the handle, and it was locked. I knocked again. "Seraphina, it's Bell. I need to talk to you."

I waited for several minutes, shifting from foot to foot and glancing along the corridor for any guards. I wasn't breaking any rules by speaking to Seraphina, but my unusual behavior would draw attention.

The bolt on the other side of the door scraped back, and Seraphina's head appeared in a small gap. "Bell, I'm busy."

"I wouldn't disturb you if this wasn't important. It's about the dragons and the stone chamber. May I come inside?"

Seraphina looked over her shoulder and scowled. "I'm not myself today."

"Are you unwell?" I asked. "Let me in, and I'll brew you a soothing tea. But I must talk to you."

She sighed. "Just a few minutes. I was about to rest. Sleep helps with the headaches."

I slid through the narrow gap, waiting until she shut and bolted the door again. She turned and stared at me. "Well? You have a question about the dragons?"

"I have information and about a million questions," I said.

"Pick your most important questions. As I said, just a few minutes." Seraphina walked carefully, her hands out as if she needed to balance herself.

I hurried over to assist her, but she brushed me away. "You may want to be seated when I tell you this news."

Seraphina was happy to slump into her favorite reading chair. She closed her eyes and massaged her forehead with her fingertips. "What news?"

I took a deep breath and then stopped. She'd think I was insane.

"Go ahead. Nothing surprises me about the dragons."

"Would the stone dragons coming back to life surprise you?"

She dropped a hand into her lap and gaped at me. "Emberthorn and Stormwing are back?"

I nodded. "Emberthorn is. Well, partially. He can sense Stormwing, too. I have so much to tell you. I don't know where to begin."

Seraphina sat forward, her gaze intense. "Tell me quickly. How do you know they're stirring?"

I paced the room before returning to her chair. "I started hearing a voice. At first, I thought it was in my head, but the voice was helping me. It began as a whisper, but then today, this morning, I discovered where the voice was coming from."

She let out a slow breath. "Emberthorn. He has the power of telecommunication. He'd use it with the other dragons when negotiating with the family. They'd talk amongst themselves to see if they could find a way forward without offending anyone. Of course, Stormwing was always encouraging him to bite off their heads and be done with it. He had no patience with the Ithric family."

Hodgepodge grumbled a laugh. "He was always my favorite dragon."

"How is this possible, though?" Seraphina asked. "In the books, there are details of how to raise the dragons again, but I've always assumed those myths were based on fairy tales."

"I've read one of those books," I said. "You heard about the robbery?"

"Oh! That was you?"

"No! Well, I was an accessory. But I read the book taken from the collection room, and I know there's a legend about bringing back the dragons with a sacrifice."

"More of an offering than a sacrifice, using Dracarys Emissary blood. But as far as I know, that's never been attempted. No one knows how dragons choose their emissary."

"We do," Hodgepodge said.

I clasped my hands in front of me. "Prince Godric just hit me, and I accidentally smeared blood on

Emberthorn. Now, he's back. Well, he's talking, blinking, and smoking. And he's insistent I'm the Dracarys Emissary who can use words of release to get him and Stormwing free. I don't know what those words are, though. Do you?"

Seraphina stared at me, open-mouthed. She lifted a shaking hand to her forehead. "You're the Dracarys Emissary?"

"No! Well, not that I know of."

Seraphina lowered her head. When she finally lifted it, there were tears on her cheeks. "I never thought this day would come. After everything I did to them, I thought we'd lost the dragons forever."

Chapter 18

"Wait! What did you do to the dragons?" I asked. "You're their friend. You're obsessed with them."

Seraphina gestured to a chair beside her, and I perched on the edge. "I... I helped the Ithric family."

"To do what?"

She pressed her hands against her mouth and breathed into them. "To weaken the dragons so they could be defeated."

Hodgepodge hissed. "Why would you do that?"

"I was promised freedom," Seraphina said. "I never fit in with my own kind, and after a vicious fight with my family, they rejected me. They sent me away as punishment. So, I lashed out."

"You know how to destroy dragons?" I couldn't hide my shock. I'd always admired Seraphina and had no clue about her harboring this dark secret.

"I was foolish and young. I believed the Ithric family's lies. They said I could have everything I desired if I helped them. They spoke the words I'd been wanting to hear from my family for such a long time. They accepted me and valued me. I was a headstrong idiot."

My heart beat at double time. "You gave the family the information they needed to capture and destroy the dragons?"

"They caught me at a weak moment when I was full of anger and hatred because I'd been denied what I deserved. I wanted to punish my family and prove I was worthy."

"You betrayed the dragons." My words came out in a horror-filled whisper.

"I did." Despair filled her tone as she hid her head in her hands. "I didn't know they'd kill them. They claimed they were fearful of the dragons. They showed me evidence to suggest Emberthorn and Stormwing were considering a takeover and wanted to eradicate the Ithric family."

"They'd never do such a thing," Hodgepodge said. "The dragons were always good to people."

"I know that now! The family must have faked the evidence so they could get the information out of me. I can't believe I fell for their lies."

"Why are you still here?" I asked. "Once you found out the family deceived you and used the information to kill the dragons, you should have left."

"I was promised freedom, but then they offered me this instead." Seraphina gestured around the vast study, full of books about dragon law and history, all of which were banned from public view. "I realized then that I had to stay and atone, undo the damage I'd caused. I've studied day and night to look for a solution. All this time, you've been right here."

I reached forward and touched her knee. Her betrayal stung, but the dragons could deal with Seraphina once they were free. "Emberthorn seems convinced I can help, but I'm not so sure. I didn't read anything about words of release in the book. Do you know how to release the dragons?"

She lifted her head, hope glittering in her tear-filled eyes. "Now I have you, I do. Your free heart means their release."

Hodgepodge hissed again. "Do not even think about taking out Bell's heart and giving it to the dragons."

Seraphina smiled. "There's no need for more sacrifice. All the dragons needed was a token offering of blood from their chosen emissary so they could return to us. And since you've given them your blood, you belong to the dragons now."

Hodgepodge stiffened against my head. "Bell is to become their slave? That's no better than her current situation. She needs to be free and safe."

"Not their slave," Seraphina said softly. "The dragons will become Bell's protectors. She's their mistress, not the other way around."

"Mother of dragons," Hodgepodge murmured.

I shook my head. "I can barely control Hodgepodge. What am I supposed to do with two great hulking dragons when they break free from their stone prisons?"

"Not just Emberthorn and Stormwing. There'll be other dragons who'll return. Once Emberthorn is free, that'll be his focus. He'll want his family back. You'll have dozens of dragons to look after."

I opened and closed my mouth several times. "I... I could clean for them. Make sure their dens are cozy. That's what I'm good at."

"You excel at so much more. Your good heart will be a guiding beacon for the dragons. And they'll need all the help they can get. After such a dark and disastrous end to their joint rule with the Ithric family, many will feel vengeful. The Ithric family is vulnerable."

"So they should be," Hodgepodge said. "They've messed up everything. This place is in chaos because of their cruel acts. They pretend this realm is productive and safe now the dragons are gone, but everyone lives in fear. Magic is prohibited to an elite few, and nearly everyone is struggling."

Seraphina nodded sadly. "The dragons will have sensed that. They were always protective of the realm. They want people to be healthy, happy, and have nothing to worry about. Many of them will be coming after the Ithric family."

"And I'm supposed to do something about that?" I couldn't. I was a follower, not a leader. "Could we do a deal? Once I get the dragons free and help the others, we'll go home and forget all about this."

Seraphina pursed her lips. "Bell, a new adventure is on your doorstep. Your quiet life may bore you after this."

"It won't! Tea and crumpets and curling up under a cozy blanket will be bliss after this is over. I want for nothing more, providing I have Hodgepodge by my side."

"We'll see about that. But first, we must attend to Emberthorn. I need to find out if he'll forgive me after my betrayal."

"What about the words of release?" I stood and followed Seraphina as she hurried to the book stacks.

"It's not a simple phrase. The words of release are combined with numerous powerful spells. Take these."

Seraphina placed several books into my hands. "It's not a case of saying 'open sesame' and Emberthorn and Stormwing return. The magic that trapped them is complicated and difficult to unpick."

"Thanks to you," Hodgepodge grumbled.

Her gaze lowered for a second. "That is something I deeply regret. I scold myself daily for my attack on the dragons. I was wrong. It should never have happened."

"But you can undo it?" I asked Seraphina.

"I've been studying for years so I can return what should never have been taken. Now I have a chance to atone. Follow me." Seraphina hurried to the door and unlocked it. She dashed into the corridor, and I had no choice but to follow her, having to jog to keep up.

"Wait! The chamber will have visitors by now. It's another ten minutes before I need to clean again," I said.

Seraphina hissed through her teeth. "This cannot wait."

"We can go through the servants' tunnel. We'll wait quietly by the door. The second the last visitor leaves, we go in and you can see Emberthorn."

Seraphina didn't look happy but followed me into the servants' tunnel then paced anxiously as the last of the visitors ambled around, unaware there was a very much alive dragon encased in the stone they were staring at.

"I can't believe this is about to happen," she whispered to me. "I've dreamed about this moment. Although I've also had nightmares about things going wrong and the dragons never coming back. You can already feel it, can't you?"

"Feel what? The dragons?" I asked.

"No, the darkness seeping into the realm."

I nodded. "Things haven't been the same since the dragons left us."

"It's more than that. Dragons are creatures of nature. They provide balance. Without them, systems slide out of control, and the barrier between the light and the dark fades. If you visit the farthest reaches of the realm, you'll find anarchy."

"I heard Prince Godric talking about an uprising."

"That's a part of it. The people farthest from the castle are less protected. The family is using excessive amounts of magic to hide the fact things are falling apart."

"You know this for a fact?" Hodgepodge asked. "You're still helping them?"

Seraphina stopped pacing. "They insist upon it. And until Bell told me Emberthorn was free, I'd lost hope of ever getting out of their clutches and righting my terrible wrong. Every day, I berate myself for my involvement in destroying the dragons."

"You know it was wrong," I said. "And you want to make amends. That counts for something."

"You'll be lucky if Emberthorn doesn't bite your head off," Hodgepodge said. "I would if I could fit your head in my mouth. I reckon it would take me at least a dozen bites to get you all."

"If that's my punishment, I'm willing to accept it," Seraphina said.

I peered through the small gap in the stone door. The last of the visitors trailed out. "Now's our chance. Let's move." I grabbed my cleaning equipment, so I had an acceptable reason for being in the chamber then hurried in first. After double-checking we were alone, I gestured for Seraphina to join us.

She ran to Emberthorn and crouched in front of him, her head down. "Forgive me. I made a terrible mistake by helping the family weaken you. I didn't know they would use my knowledge to destroy you. They told me you were unstable and planned a takeover. They lied. I should never have trusted them."

"Not just me, but all of us," Emberthorn's voice grumbled out.

Seraphina rested a trembling hand on Emberthorn's right foot. "I was young and thought I knew better. They claimed a dark faction had appeared among the dragons, poisoning minds. They had to stop it. And it made sense, since my family rejected me."

"Your family has strict rules. You broke them. Punishment had to be expected."

She lifted her head. "I made a huge mistake. And I had my head turned by honeyed lies."

"What connection does your family have with dragons?" I asked. "Have you always been their scholars?"

Seraphina didn't speak, simply stared at Emberthorn. It was as if they were silently communicating.

"That is a story for another time," Emberthorn finally said. "I believe Seraphina wishes to make amends."

"I do!" Seraphina remained on her knees.

"Bell, if you get any hint of betrayal, I permit your companion to incinerate her," Emberthorn said.

I jerked my head back. "You want Hodgie to kill Seraphina? He's more of a lazy fireside snoozer than a lethal predator."

"I predate when I have to," Hodgepodge said. "You should have seen me during the recent locust plague. I ate so many, I could barely move. Bell rolled me home, and I slept for a week."

Emberthorn grumbled a laugh. "You are a worthy companion. If you needed to, you could stop anything that threatened Bell."

I hated the idea of Hodgepodge killing. He was incredible at ensuring our room stayed spider and bug free, but ending Seraphina's life?

"I will never betray you again," Seraphina said. "I'll be your humble servant for eternity."

Emberthorn grunted, not mollified by her words.

I glanced at the door. Time wasn't on our side. "What are the next steps?"

"The release magic takes weeks to work," Seraphina said. "And we'll need to be careful not to get caught applying the runes and potions."

"Weeks! We won't have that if anyone from the castle realizes the dragons are stirring," I said.

A guard yanked open the door, making me tense. "Bell, there's been a disturbance out here, so we're closing the chamber to visitors until we get things under control. Someone reckoned they'd seen a ghost, so the crowd panicked. Idiots."

I forced a smile. "Perfect. We're doing some specialist cleaning on the statues. How long have we got?"

"A few hours. Lady Isolda is angry because a runaway visitor got up to the family rooms. Claimed they were looking for the bathroom. Heads will roll if we don't fix this fast." The guard vanished, and the door slammed.

"Luck is on our side," Seraphina said.

Astrid appeared out of the servants' tunnels. "Godric is on the move. He's leaving the castle and going to the docks. The women are being transported this morning. If we're getting them free, we need to act now."

Chapter 19

I had no choice but to leave Emberthorn and Seraphina together. She didn't have long to work on the release magic, and I didn't trust her, not after she'd betrayed the dragons, but she'd been truly repentant, and Emberthorn assured me she was no longer a threat.

Astrid tugged on my arm. "It's now or never. This is our only chance to rescue the women before the ship sets sail and we lose our chance."

"Go," Emberthorn murmured. "If Seraphina misbehaves, she'll have you and Hodgepodge to answer to."

I nodded, shot Seraphina a warning look, and then hurried out with Astrid.

We sped out of the castle and saw Warwick accompanying Prince Godric. The prince strutted around as if waiting for applause because he was up before sundown. Then he climbed into a waiting horse and carriage with a steam powered backup engine infused with magic. Even when magic was freely used, that mode of transport had been a luxury few could afford.

"We need our own transport or we'll lose them," I said.

"I've got you," Astrid said. "Be back in a few minutes."

"We don't have a few minutes," Hodgepodge said. "They're on the move."

"Unless you want to use magic to transport us to the docks, you have to trust me." Astrid raised an eyebrow. "Do you trust me, Hodgie baby?"

Hodgepodge huffed at her. "Go get us a ride."

She laughed as she jogged away.

I paced from foot to foot. I still lacked a plan for how we'd get the women off the ship without revealing everything we knew to Prince Godric. Maybe we had to reveal ourselves, and then I'd figure everything else out after we were on the run.

"Stop fretting," Hodgepodge murmured from the snug pocket in my underskirt. "We'll get to the women in time. And when we return, maybe we'll have a dragon free."

"Can we trust Seraphina to do the right thing?"

"She will. There's something about her that makes my scales itch."

"That doesn't sound good." I glanced around, waiting for Astrid to return.

"In a good way. When she was staring at Emberthorn, I'm sure they were communicating."

"I felt that, too. There was a weird energy in the room. Maybe her family could telepathically link with the dragons. Some dragons speak to each other in that way."

"Seraphina will come through for Emberthorn and Stormwing. And once we have them back, they can figure out the rest. We'll return home and forget we ever went on this quest to awaken two dragons and stop Prince Godric's sleazy plans."

I hoped it would be that simple.

A horn honked, and Astrid pulled up in a magical, steam-powered motorbike with a sidecar that had a slash of silver paint down the side. She tossed me a helmet.

"Is this thing safe?" I clambered into the sidecar and arranged my skirt so Hodgepodge could sit comfortably between my legs.

"Not the last time I checked. Hold tight. She flies like the wind." Astrid pressed a button, steam billowed around us, and the vehicle shot off. We zoomed along the road behind the carriage, keeping a safe distance.

My teeth rattled as we went over bumps and avoided crashing into startled-looking passersby.

"Where did you get this thing from?" I asked.

"I built it. Keeps me busy in my spare time and out of trouble."

I focused on the carriage and not on my bones being bruised. The horses pulling Prince Godric's carriage kept up a fast trot, suggesting he was keen to get the evidence of his misdeeds quickly out to sea. "What did you hear about the ship?"

"I didn't get much detail. Warwick passed on a message through the kitchen staff. He overheard Prince Godric having a private conversation with his brother. They were arguing as usual."

"I got the impression Prince Jasper doesn't agree with what he's doing."

"They've fought since they were children. They're still children, just in men's bodies. If one of them wants to do something, the other one doesn't. Idiots. Anyway, Warwick said we needed to move now."

"Can't you keep this thing steady?" Hodgepodge asked. "I'm getting sick."

"I don't look after the roads, sweetie pie. We'll be there soon."

I gently patted Hodgepodge in an attempt to settle him as I clung to the door handle.

The carriage occasionally had to slow when there was someone in the way, but as soon as they saw it was a royal carriage, they were swift to move. Everyone knew better than to face Prince Godric's wrath.

Half an hour later, I got a briny, salty whiff of sea air, and I caught glimpses of folded sails and other nautical equipment I couldn't name.

Astrid tucked the bike behind a stack of wooden pallets and killed the engine. "We walk from here. Less conspicuous."

"I don't call that monstrosity inconspicuous. All the prince's guards will have seen us." Hodgepodge flopped onto the ground, his eyes closed as he breathed in and out.

"They're too busy pandering to the prince. And she's dynamite on the roads. She's gotten me out of plenty of scrapes." Astrid tucked away our helmets. "Let's see what our charmless prince is up to, shall we?"

I collected Hodgepodge and tucked him back into my underskirt. I didn't know how dock workers and sailors would feel about seeing him. I'd heard tales that they traded in exotic goods, and I didn't want anyone to think Hodgepodge may be worth trading and steal him.

We maintained a discreet distance behind Prince Godric as he walked with his guards through the docks. Everyone acknowledged him with a bow or a curtsy as he strutted past.

"The ship he's got the women on is called the Mermaid Tail," Astrid murmured. "Look out for it."

"We need to get on that ship," I said.

Astrid slid me some serious side-eye. "What are you planning to do, sail away and out of Prince Godric's grasp?"

"Don't get cold feet on me now. I got the gang together for just this reason. We're getting those women free."

"How?"

"I'm... I'm working on it."

"You don't know, do you?"

I looked around. "Still working on it."

Astrid shrugged. "I've always thought a life at sea would be fun. Freedom, no ties, and if you arrive at a place you don't like, you haul anchor and leave after taking all the useful plunder you can grab."

"If you can handle the seasickness," Hodgepodge muttered.

"True. Not all of us have legs or stomachs made for the open water." Astrid tensed. "Evander's here."

I nodded. I knew he'd been skulking around the docks for any sign of the ship. He was lounging against a brick building, looking half-asleep, one foot resting on the wall and a hat partially concealing his face. He barely acknowledged us, other than a faint downward tilt of his chin.

We wandered over casually and stood close to him.

"It's the ship with the green sails," he said, not looking at us.

"Have you been on board?" I whispered.

"Not yet. Griffin is on there, though. And a group of women were led onboard half an hour ago. One of them tried to escape, and she was knocked out. They're in a bad way. Most of them had to be carried on."

Astrid hissed an angry breath. "We need to get a look."

Evander glanced at us from under his hat. "Griffin will report back soon. I said I should snoop because I can sneak in and out of anywhere better than him, but he insisted."

"I can sneak better than you," Astrid said.

"With your pretty face, they might decide to take you with them. I'll go see how he's doing. Make sure he hasn't gotten himself caught and tossed overboard." Evander smirked and strolled away, quickly merging into the bustle of the dock. I looked around to see if I could spot where he'd gone, but it was as if he'd vanished.

"Evander uses illegal magic," Astrid said. "That's how he gets away with so much."

I nodded, but maintained my silence. We waited for ten anxious minutes, only punctuating the time by buying apples for breakfast and keeping out of sight as much as possible.

Evander appeared again as if out of thin air, his expression set grim. "It's bad news. I overheard scummy Godric questioning the captain about where the women would be sent and what would happen if a few got lost at sea. Apparently, our charming prince thinks it would be no loss for them to disappear before the ship docked at its next destination."

Astrid bared her teeth. "He's evil."

"Where are they being held?" I asked.

"Below deck. I don't think the sailors consider them a threat because they're not tied up, just shut in the hold. I didn't get a good look at all of them, but they seem weak. Some are unconscious," Evander said.

I studied the ship as sailors strode on and off, loading cargo and supplies. "Take me onboard as your prisoner."

Evander's eyes widened. "You don't know how to fight. And you're a terrible liar. They'll see you don't belong."

"We need to get a good look around. It's no good using Astrid. She's too well known."

Astrid smirked. "My reputation is excellent, and it always precedes me."

"Prince Godric knows you," Hodgepodge said, his voice muffled in my skirt.

"He won't remember me. Well, he may think I'm familiar, but he'll be so preoccupied with erasing evidence of his guilt that he won't make the connection. He rarely notices servants."

"You're wrong. He'll know you," Hodgepodge said. "Don't do it."

"If he remembers our interactions, you can jump on his face and bite him. Give me time to escape."

Hodgepodge growled. "I'll take great pleasure in biting him."

Evander didn't look happy but finally nodded. "If you get into a mess, I may not be able to bail you out."

I felt in my pockets, reassured as my fingers brushed the ring of strength and the wind summoner Elara had given me. "Let's do this before I lose my nerve."

"We'll have to make this quick." Evander held my elbow. "Godric was talking to the captain on the other side of the ship when I was there, so we should be able to get you on without him seeing."

"Good luck," Astrid whispered. "I'll be right behind you."

We strode to the ship, my heart racing as we walked up the boarding ramp. I kept my gaze lowered.

"I've got a late arrival," Evander said. "She got left behind."

I kept my head down, only able to see booted feet.

"Put her in the hold with the rest of them," a sailor said.

Evander strode off, taking me with him.

"What in all blazes are you doing here?" Warwick's angry hiss reached my ears.

My head whipped up, and I came eye to eye with his shocked fury.

"I'm here to receive fair payment for delivering another troublemaker." Evander grinned as he played his part. "And before you explode with anger, this crazy move was Bell's idea."

Warwick glowered at me. "Are you insane?"

"I might be. But I have to get to the women. I can convince them to fight back."

He shook his head. "They can barely stand, let alone fight. Evander, get her out of here before Prince Godric notices."

"Fix everything down. It's almost time to leave," someone yelled.

"I have to get to the women," I said.

Warwick looked over my head then pulled a blade from his belt and handed it to me. "I won't be able to protect you."

"I can protect myself," I said. "But if you've got my back when trouble arises, I'll appreciate it."

Warwick sighed, his glare flicking to Evander.

Evander stepped back, his hands raised. "Bell's in charge. She wanted to get on the ship, so I made it happen. The rest is up to her."

Warwick heaved out another sigh. "Be prepared for anything. We sail in five minutes."

Chapter 20

I'd only been below deck with Hodgepodge for ten minutes and already felt queasy. The floor rocked beneath my feet as I huddled against the side of the ship. Warwick had placed me in the hold with the other women, and although my first instinct was to talk to them, they were so scared and weak that I didn't want to overwhelm them.

Hodgepodge growled and shuffled in my underskirt, and I got the sense he felt queasy, too. He softly cursed the waves, but I hushed him into silence.

I looked at the woman who was slumped beside me. "Hey, are you okay?"

She barely lifted her head.

I inspected the other women in the group. Maggie was among them and so was Sacha, my missing cleaning companion, both out cold on the floor. The others were unconscious or barely had their eyes open. There was only one woman who caught my eye. She was short, round, in her forties, and had a mess of curly dark hair.

"What happened to all of you?" I asked her.

"Before we were brought here, Prince Godric was taking our blood. Apparently, he wanted a backup supply," she said quietly. "The guy's lost his mind. He's been taking our blood for weeks."

"Do you know what he wants it for?"

"As if he'd tell us anything." Her brow furrowed. "You weren't in the dungeon with us. Why are you here?"

I drew in a breath to explain but paused when the hatch opened. A group of sailors came down. Their lewd looks turned my stomach.

"I told you we had special cargo," one of them said to his friend, jabbing him in the ribs. "Which one do you like the look of?"

The woman I'd been talking to pulled herself to her feet and moved to the front of the group. "Mind your business. We're not here for you."

"Says who?" the mouthy sailor frowned at her, and his gaze drifted over her figure. "You're too old for me, anyway."

"Show some respect, sonny. Didn't your mother teach you manners?" She rested her hands on her broad hips.

"Get out of my way." He shoved her in the shoulder, and she staggered to one side.

I rose and caught her before she lost her balance and hit the floor.

The sailor grinned at me. "You'll do. You're better preserved."

"I'm going nowhere with you."

He chuckled. "We can stay here if you'd like an audience. Doesn't bother me."

"What's going on?" Heavy footsteps clamped down the steps, and a long-haired, tattooed sailor in a scruffy uniform appeared. "You're not supposed to be down here."

"We were told to check the supplies. That's what we're doing." The crude sailor rubbed his hands together, still looking at me.

"Get your filthy mind out of the gutter and go back on deck where you're supposed to be. The ship is active. That means you're on duty."

"Can't we have fun? There's nothing to do until we hit open water."

"These women belong to Prince Godric." The tattooed sailor marched closer. "Do you want to explain to him what happened to them on this voyage?"

"Captain says they won't make it to the other side," another sailor grumbled. "No one will know."

He received a whack on the back of the head for that comment. "These are people's daughters or sisters. Think about your own family and how you'd like them treated if they were in this position."

"My sister would never be so stupid as to get herself in a mess like this," the moody sailor said.

"On deck, now, or you'll receive lashes," the scruffily uniformed sailor ordered.

The men glared at each other and then walked up the wooden steps, grumbling to themselves.

The sailor who'd helped us looked around the hold. "You won't be bothered again, ladies. My apologies. This isn't the regular ship's crew, and it appears they don't know how to behave. I'll watch over the hold."

I stepped forward. "Thanks. Can you tell us where we're going?"

A flicker of sadness crossed his face. "It's best you don't know."

"Has Prince Godric paid the captain to throw us overboard?" I asked.

A few of the women whimpered when I said that.

"I shouldn't tell you."

"Please, if there's anything you can do to help..." I reached for his arm, but he stepped back.

"I'm sorry. The best I can do is make sure you're not poorly treated until the captain makes a decision."

"How much was he paid to murder us?" the curly-haired woman who'd stood up to the sailors said.

The tattooed sailor shook his head. "I wish things could be different." He turned, stomped up the stairs, and closed the hatch.

"Coward," the woman muttered.

"He helped us," I said.

"Only to watch us get tossed into the sea. That's what Prince Godric wants. I've seen how he operates, so I know he's twisted enough to go through with it."

I tilted my head. "I know you. You ran the tavern at the end of Brick Lane. Dolores... um, I forget your surname."

"I did! Dolores Nickel. And I ran it well for years until Prince Godric got it in his head to abduct local women for his sick fantasies. Taking our blood. The man has lost his marbles. There were always rumors of mental instability among that family. Some say it was because of inbreeding, and I can well believe it."

I watched her closely for a few seconds. "It's not because of that."

Dolores settled her arms over her chest. "What would you know? You weren't in the dungeon, and I don't remember you coming into my tavern."

I smiled. "That's my superpower. I'm invisible. Bell Blackthorn. I work in the castle, cleaning the stone chamber. One of the key parts of my job is to stay out of sight of visitors. I keep the chamber spotless while making sure I'm never seen."

"Oh! You look after the stone dragons?" Dolores sighed. "I sure miss those guys."

It was now or never. "You won't have to miss them for much longer. Prince Godric's been taking your blood because he believes he can get the dragons back with the right blood sacrifice."

"Hah! I knew he was crazy!"

"Prince Godric had the right idea, but he was picking the wrong women. And... the dragons are coming back. Emberthorn is awake."

Dolores was silent for a second then burst out laughing. "You must have whacked your head on the way in."

"The Ithric family has the dragons' bones inside their stone statues. Magic kept them constrained, but Prince Godric hit me, and my blood ended up on Emberthorn. It woke him."

"Why is your blood so special?" she asked. "I thought you said you were a cleaner."

"I... I am. But I have a bond with the dragons."

"What you have is a fantastical mind. The dragons are gone. This realm is in chaos, and it won't be long before there's a full-scale war. The family is falling apart, and Prince Godric's actions show how desperate he's become. Murderous little psycho."

"Listen to Bell." Hodgepodge hopped out of my underskirt, causing Dolores to rear back in alarm and swat at him. "I've seen it all. Prince Godric's crazy behavior, trapping women, and then Emberthorn returning. He's still trapped in stone form, but it won't be long before we have dragons soaring through the skies again."

Dolores quickly recovered herself. "If he looks anything like you, we'll be disappointed."

I gathered Hodgepodge into my arms as he hissed. "We have to get back to shore. Which means we need to get control of the ship. Who's with me? If we get home, we'll be safe. The dragons won't let the Ithric family hurt us, and Prince Godric will have to answer for his crimes." I looked around the hold, but the women who were awake didn't meet my gaze. "If we work together, we can get free. I've got friends on board. They can get the ship turned around."

"I admire your spirit," Dolores said.

"You'll help?" I asked.

She let slip a sigh. "We're dead, anyway. Why not give them a taste of their own medicine?"

"I'll help, too." Evander appeared from out of the shadows. "Astrid is on deck with Warwick. And Griffin is lurking somewhere. Bell, you have an army of skilled warriors at your disposal."

"Evander Thorne! I might have known you'd be mixed up in this muddle." Dolores hurried over and kissed his cheek. "Of all the ships, you sneak onto this one."

"I can never resist your charms, Dolores." He bowed over her hand and kissed it, making her blush.

"He's on our side," I said.

"Bell is in charge, though," Evander said. "She thinks she can save you, so I'd trust her."

Dolores arched a brow. "What other option do we have?"

Evander pressed a finger to his lips and disappeared back into the shadows. A second later, the hatch opened, and footsteps crept down. The crude sailor was back, and his sights were set on me.

I hid Hodgepodge in my skirts and stood my ground as he approached, rubbing his hands together again.

"Back so soon?" I asked.

"How could I resist such charm?" He grinned at me. "Besides, Mattius is being yelled at by the captain, which left you unguarded. I took that as a sign to collect my due."

"You're owed nothing from me."

"Leave her alone," Dolores said.

"I've already warned you to hold your tongue, hag. Now, let's have a little fun together before the captain notices I'm missing." He stepped closer and grabbed my face, leaning in for an unwelcome kiss.

Before his lips met mine, his eyes bulged, and he yelped. He staggered away. Hodgepodge was attached to his groin.

He yelped again. "What the hell is this thing? It's biting me!"

Dolores roared with laughter as the sailor hopped around, attempting to dislodge Hodgepodge from his crown jewels. But Hodgepodge was like a pit bull. When he got his teeth sunk in, he didn't let go until he wanted to.

The sailor clutched his groin and hopped around some more, leaving droplets of blood on the wooden floor. He was only silenced when Evander stepped out from the shadows and whacked him over the back of the head, and he slumped to the ground, unconscious.

"I take that as our sign," Dolores said. "Come on, girls. Any of you who can stand and fight, it's time for payback."

Several women staggered to their feet, their eyes wide with shock, although several of them looked excited about getting revenge.

"The coast is clear," Evander said from the top of the wooden steps. "Up we go, ladies."

I slipped the ring of strength onto my finger and then gently dislodged Hodgepodge from the sailor's groin. "Good boy."

"No one disrespects you and gets away with it," he said. "Let's see who else we can bite."

There were six of us, Dolores assisting and encouraging the other women on the stairs. Evander took the lead and led us onto the swaying deck.

"Hey! Those women shouldn't be out. And who are you?" What must have been the captain strode toward us. Several of his crewmates followed, drinks in hand, not concerned by our arrival.

"They needed fresh air," Evander said. "Nothing worse than having an upset stomach in the hold."

"I don't care what they need. I was paid to keep them below deck. And you haven't answered my question." The captain looked at Evander with suspicion. "Who the hell are you?"

"My apologies for not introducing myself." Evander swept into a bow. "I'm the savior of lost women. The un-doer of dark deeds caused by the Ithric family. But if you pay me enough, I can be charming, too."

The captain grunted. "What you are is an idiot. Prince Godric, do you know this guy?"

The breath was knocked from my lungs. I hadn't expected Prince Godric to still be on board.

"What are you yelling about?" Prince Godric's irritated tone sounded close by, sending a flood of icy fear sliding through my veins.

"This man says he has something to do with you. He's not a member of my crew. I don't like unauthorized passengers aboard. You should have told me you were bringing someone else."

"I don't know what you're twittering about. I only brought my guards," Prince Godric said.

I glanced at Evander. We shared a nod. Then I looked at the women. "Ready?"

Dolores cracked her knuckles. "It's payback time."

The women surged toward the sailors, catching many of them off-guard. The salty sea air stung my nostrils as the ship hit a wave, and I stumbled back. My heart raced as a burly sailor, his eyes bloodshot, lurched toward me with a menacing grin. He swung a heavy fist at me, but I ducked just in time. I felt the rush of air as his fist whizzed past my head.

I extended my hand in a clumsy chopping motion and hit the guy's throat. He flew back before crumpling to the deck. There was no time to celebrate my victory or how incredible the ring's power was as chaos erupted when more sailors noticed the commotion. Bottles crashed, and curses filled the air.

Hodgepodge flipped out of my skirt and growled, his thick tail slashing from side to side.

A sailor charged at me with a broken bottle. I parried his attack with a shove and a swift kick to his chest, sending him tumbling backward into the arms of his companions.

Hodgepodge lunged at another sailor, his jaws snapping shut inches from the man's throat. The sailor screamed and stumbled back, tripping over his own feet.

"We can't best them with our fists, but I've got something that'll stop them," Dolores yelled at me. "Girls, with me. Bell, you keep doing what you're doing."

The women stopped fighting and formed a circle, a haunting incantation filling the air. Dolores was in the center as their voices rose above the chaos. A shimmering barrier of energy formed, protecting us from the sailors' onslaught.

I locked eyes with the tattooed sailor who'd helped us when some of the crew had come calling. He stood at the helm, a determined expression on his face. He held my gaze and nodded. With a wave of his hand, he summoned a swirling vortex of water from the ocean. The water shot up, drenching the nearest sailors and knocking them off their feet.

Another wave of sailors appeared, and the chaos continued. I drew back with Hodgepodge, but just as I thought we might be overwhelmed, a burst of magic erupted from behind me. I turned to see Evander and Astrid, their faces determined as they stood together.

I grabbed the wind summoner from my pocket and tossed it to Evander. He checked it over then blew a sharp note, and a gust of wind swirled around him. He directed the tempest toward a group of oncoming sailors, sending them tumbling and disoriented. With a flick of his wrist, he summoned a wall of water, creating a barrier between us and the advancing mob.

Astrid, her eyes blazing with fiery magic, stepped forward. Flames danced along her fingertips as she sent fireballs hurtling toward the sailors who dared to challenge us. The flames erupted upon impact, sending our attackers scrambling to douse the flames that clung to their clothes. Several pitched overboard.

A sailor charged at me from the side, but before I could react, a burst of Evander's magic sent the man sprawling to the deck. I nodded my thanks, and he gave me a cheeky smile.

Astrid's fireballs continued to rain down on the sailors, forcing them to retreat and regroup. Their faces were twisted in fear and frustration as they realized they'd underestimated our combined powers.

I sought Warwick and noticed him at the back of the ship, facing us, his blade drawn and his sparking staff glowing. He must be defending Prince Godric. Of course, he needed to assume a veneer of loyalty to avoid suspicion.

Blades clashed, and I turned to see Griffin in fierce combat with two sword wielding sailors.

"You! I know you! Get out of my way. I know that witch. Let me pass or I'll have your head."

My heart froze as Prince Godric's harsh tone grew closer. The sailors stopped their attack on Griffin, and even the women stopped chanting. Warwick strode beside the prince, his expression grimly determined, although an apology flashed in his eyes.

"What are you doing here?" Prince Godric's cold glare was spearing onto me. "You're the freak obsessed with the dragons. You work in my castle."

It was too late to hide, so I stood firm. "Obsessed or not, I'm helping those women you've had trapped in the dungeon."

Prince Godric barked a laugh. "A freak and insane. You can't stand against me."

My gaze flicked around the ship. "If that's true, then why am I here? And why are the women almost free?"

"I'll have your head for this." Prince Godric lunged at me, knocking me off balance, and I hit the side of the ship.

Hodgepodge flew at Prince Godric, aiming for his throat. His tail wrapped around the prince's head, and he hissed in his face.

Warwick and several of the women cried out a warning as Prince Godric grabbed me. His weight unbalanced me and my feet slipped. I grabbed for anything to keep me from falling and dug my fingers into his embroidered tunic, but it wasn't enough to stop my fall over the side and toward the icy gray waves.

Chapter 21

I hit the water, still entangled in Prince Godric's painful grasp. The waves were freezing, and the salt stung my eyes as I went under. I kicked hard, landing a blow on Prince Godric's thigh, and he let go.

I stayed under the water, swimming as fast as I could. Where was Hodgepodge? He'd jumped on Prince Godric just before we went overboard, but I didn't see what happened when he hit the water. I shot up to the surface and sucked in air. I was close to the ship, and Astrid was looking overboard. I raised a hand, but she didn't see me.

A gasp left my lips as my heavy, waterlogged clothing threatened to drag me under. I spun in a fast circle, looking for Hodgepodge and Prince Godric. There was no sign of the prince, but Hodgepodge lay flat on the water's surface, his wings splayed. I splashed over to him and lifted him up.

He blinked at me and hissed. "I hate the sea. Millions of fish swimming around in this muck, peeing and defecating. That's what we're swimming in. A fish toilet!"

I choked out a laugh and held him close. "Anything broken?"

"No. But I'm not a natural swimmer. I was able to stay afloat by spreading my wings. How about you?"

"A few bruises, but nothing bad. We should swim back to the ship."

"What about our scummy prince? Did he resurface?"

"I lost sight of him when we went under. Maybe he can't swim."

"Let's hope a pack of marauding killer whales dragged him down and are playing with him."

"So long as they don't come back and play with us, I'm fine with that as an end to his life." I started a one-handed swim back toward the ship, my movements slow with my sodden clothing clinging to me and Hodgepodge balanced on my outstretched arm.

I yelped as a hand wrapped around my ankle and pulled me under. I tried to keep hold of Hodgepodge but lost my grip as I was pulled down and came face to face with Prince Godric.

Rage surged through me, not just at Prince Godric, but at everything he represented. The cruelty, the oppression, the pain he'd caused to so many innocent people. I refused to let him win. I touched the ring on my finger.

A powerful blast of magic erupted from the ring, pushing Prince Godric away from me and creating a brief opening for escape. I kicked my legs and swam toward the surface. Gasping for air, I broke through the water.

Prince Godric was right behind me. As he closed in on me, sparks of magic dancing around him, I gathered the last bit of strength within me and summoned my own magic. I focused my anger, fear, and determination into a single spell. A beam of light shot from my hands, colliding with Prince Godric's magic in a dazzling display of power.

Surprise crossed his face then he snarled. "You're dead! You're fighting your future king and using illegal magic. Every court in this land will find you guilty and hang you from the gate post by your neck so the peasants will mock you."

Our magic clashed and swirled across the water. His hatred and malice were clear in every move he made, and I fought with all the love and hope I had for the people he'd hurt. The water churned around us, and the air crackled with energy.

Prince Godric unleashed another wave of magic, sending a barrage of ice shards toward me. I deflected the shards with an efficiency I didn't know I had in me. The ring must have more power than Elara let on.

With a sneer, Prince Godric conjured dark clouds. Lightning crackled through the sky, and he directed it at me. The lightning struck the water, but I dove under the waves, avoiding a direct hit.

We couldn't keep this up, but Prince Godric seemed to draw strength from his anger and desperation as more lightning strikes hit the waves, looking for a target. I channeled my love for my friends and my people and focused it, summoning a powerful beam of light, brighter and more intense than any I had ever created. The beam shot toward Prince Godric from beneath the water, and he raised his hands to shield himself. It collided with his dark magic, and for a moment, there was a blinding clash of colors.

I poured everything I had into that spell, pushing my body and my magic way beyond their natural limits. Prince Godric let out a scream as the light engulfed him. I kept the beam going, not giving him a chance to recover.

He tossed out a spell that hit me with a darkly unpleasant thud, and my magic faded as I plunged under the water, my spine shuddering. I surfaced again just in time to hear a growling rumble of thunder overhead, and more dark clouds piled one on top of the other, blotting out the light.

Where was Hodgepodge? My heart stuttered as my gaze landed on his floating form, and I swam over to him.

"You have got to get me swimming lessons," he grumbled when he saw me floundering toward him. "I'm no use to you like this."

I was almost within arm's reach when a blast of brilliant lightning smashed down on top of Hodgepodge. I screamed, blinded by the light, and powerless to help him as he went under the waves.

I dove, desperate to save him, but I found no sign of him. I swam to the spot where I'd last seen him and swirled around, but it was gloomy and the waves choppy, and I could see nothing. I thrust out several light balls, illuminating the darkness. He wasn't there.

After grabbing a breath, I dove again. I kept going, grabbing air and ignoring the freezing conditions and stinging salt as I searched for my best friend. Hodgepodge couldn't be gone. He was a part of me. Without him, I couldn't go on. He gave me a reason to get up in the mornings, to smile, and to seek those tiny moments of joy in an often difficult, gray world.

I resurfaced again, and an arm wrapped around me from behind and choked me. I grabbed it and dug my nails in, but the grip was solid.

"You dare to go up against me?" Prince Godric snarled in my ear. "I'll make you sorry you were ever born."

I wheezed out a breath and attempted to elbow him in the ribs, but it had no effect. He was so full of rage that I doubted anything I could do would stop him. I needed to get free so I could use the ring's power against him and return to search for Hodgepodge.

As my breath faded and my strength waned, I found satisfaction in knowing Prince Godric had failed. Even if I was gone, my friends would save the women and take them back to their loved ones. They'd be safe. And Prince Godric's twisted efforts would be revealed to the realm and the dragons. Seraphina was working to bring back Emberthorn, and he'd soon punish this broken prince and his deranged family.

Darkness clouded my vision, and my head slipped beneath the water.

Something huge rose up, sending a massive wave of water over me, taking me under with Prince Godric. I'd only gotten a glimpse of whatever sea beast it was, but it was mottled brown with large ridged plates running down its spine. I'd rather be eaten by a sea creature than choked to death by Prince Godric, so I kicked back at him several times as we struggled under the water. The grip around my neck slackened, and I pushed away.

I turned to land a blow using the ring of strength, but Prince Godric was fleeing, swimming away from me with speed. I twisted in the water, and my gaze lifted. A giant, mottled dragon-like creature hovered in the air. It had a massive snout and rows of razor-sharp teeth exposed as it snarled. There was a distinctive red leathery ruff around its neck, which was fully on display.

I blinked the salt out of my eyes. "Hodgepodge?"

He tipped one giant wing in acknowledgment then opened his mouth and breathed an enormous blast of fire toward Prince Godric.

The last sound I heard from Prince Godric was him yelling in terror before the flames covered him. I was so stunned that I almost forgot to swim and slipped under the water. Before I went too far, huge claws scooped me out, and I was brought up to Hodgepodge's snout.

I rested my hands on his scales. His beautiful, bronzed, enormous scales. "What happened to you? I thought you died when the lightning hit you."

He grumbled several times as if clearing his throat, and a plume of smoke came out of his nose, almost blinding me. "Sorry, this is a lot to handle."

I waved away the smoke, choking on it for a few seconds. "No kidding. You look amazing. I'm so glad you're not hurt."

"The lightning didn't hurt me. I felt this surge of power when I was under the water. It was like being tickled all over, and then I turned into this! And breathing fire is incredible. I barbecued Prince Godric in seconds."

I turned in Hodgepodge's huge claws and looked out over the waves. There was no sign of Prince Godric, but he couldn't have survived that blistering attack.

"Is this how you're going to stay?" I asked Hodgepodge as he clumsily flapped his wings.

His eyes widened. "I'll never fit in your underskirt if I stay this size."

I laughed and kissed his snout. "And new lodgings. I'll need to find you somewhere to live."

"You'll stay with me, though? I know I look scary—"

"Hodgepodge! You're not scary. You're beautiful. You'd be beautiful to me, whatever size or shape you are. Don't worry. We'll figure things out. If we need to find a new home, then we will. And I'll make sure there's plenty of room for you," I reassured him as I scratched under his chin, having to use both hands.

"As long as we're together, I won't mind if we live in a cave. So long as it's warm and there are cookies and comfy places to sit."

"Where did the lightning magic come from?" I asked. "That wasn't your average bolt of light. Did someone see we were in trouble and lend a hand?"

"I have no clue, but I need to thank them. If I hadn't changed, I wouldn't have been able to save your life," he replied with purring approval as I kept scratching him.

"You'd have figured out how to save me, whatever size you were," I said.

"Hey! Is that mighty beast Hodgepodge?" Astrid yelled from the ship as it approached us.

I waved. "It is!"

Evander appeared next to Astrid. "Looking good, lizard. We've secured the ship. The crew won't cause us any more trouble."

Hodgepodge flapped his wings, moving closer to the ship in a jerky movement as he learned how to use his enormous new flappers.

"Did anyone get hurt?" I asked.

"Only the idiot sailors who put up a fight." Warwick joined them, along with Griffin.

"What happened to Hodgepodge?" Griffin asked.

"Something magical," I said.

"We're turning the ship around and heading to shore," Astrid said. "Want to hop aboard? Although Hodgepodge will need to fly or we'll capsize."

"The tide is against you," Hodgepodge said. "Attach ropes to me, and I'll pull you back. We'll be there in half the time."

"I'm staying with you," I said. "Is it okay if I ride on your back?"

He lifted me, and I settled against one of the large raised ridges behind his ruff. It was a perfectly comfortable seat, and it would be easy to fashion a comfy saddle to use so I could ride with Hodgepodge, assuming he stayed in this form. I had a lot of questions I needed answered, but now wasn't the time. We had to get the women home.

Within ten minutes, Hodgepodge had hold of a number of ropes secured around the ship and had turned it, and we were heading to shore.

I sat on the back of my new giant wyvern friend in a state of stunned silence. We'd completed our quest. The women Prince Godric had exploited and misused were safe. He'd been defeated, and his misdeeds were about to be revealed to all.

But somehow, this didn't feel over.

Chapter 22

I yawned so widely my jaw cracked. I smacked my lips together and smiled. I'd had the most blissful slumber. And after the high adventures of yesterday, I'd deserved it.

After docking the ship, we'd discreetly returned the women to their homes, and everyone else slipped off to act as if nothing odd had happened. Evander and Astrid sidled away together, bickering as usual. Warwick had returned to the family. Griffin had gone back to his work in the yard, and I'd returned to cleaning my dragons, just making it in time before the guards re-opened the chamber to visitors.

When I'd gotten back to the chamber, there'd been no sign of Seraphina, and Emberthorn was back in his stone state.

I yawned again. As much as I wanted to stay in my cozy bed, I needed to see Hodgepodge. When he'd gotten close enough to the shore, we'd cut the ropes loose, he'd set me on the deck, and flown away. Until I figured out exactly how long he'd stay super-sized, I couldn't risk anyone seeing him. They'd get excited and think the dragons had returned.

I'd just rolled out of bed when there was a knock on my front door. I pulled on clothing and hurried to open it a crack. Astrid, Evander, Griffin, and Warwick stood outside.

Astrid grinned. "I told you she'd be sleeping."

"It's my day off!" I said.

"Let us in, lazybones," Evander said. "We have things to celebrate."

"I told them not to bother you," Warwick said gruffly. "But as usual, they never listen to sense."

Griffin smiled at me. "Any news about Hodgepodge?"

"He was good when I left him last night." I opened the door wider and let them in. "I found him a place in the woods. No one will find him, and he was as exhausted as I was, so I'm hoping he slept the whole night through. I was about to visit him."

"A celebration first." Evander set down two large bottles of cherry brandy. "Gifts from Dolores. She's grateful to be back bossing people around and kicking out drunks."

"It's not even eight in the morning." Astrid rolled her eyes.

"I brought something more suitable from the bakery." Warwick set down a large white box.

"I'll make the coffee." Griffin headed into the kitchen and got to work.

Astrid grinned. "I just brought myself. How are you feeling after yesterday?"

"I'm not convinced I didn't dream the whole thing." I peeked inside the bakery box and selected an apricot pastry.

Evander grabbed mugs and filled them with generous slugs of cherry brandy. "It was real. We went up against Prince Godric, and you beat him."

"I have Hodgepodge to thank for defeating him. And all of you. I could never have saved those women if you didn't help me."

"We await our payment," Evander said.

Astrid elbowed him in the ribs.

He winced but then grinned. "Okay. This was a freebie. Just don't tell anyone else I do good deeds, or I'll have a long line of desperate people outside my door begging for charity. And I don't do charity."

Warwick took his own pastry. "People have been asking where Prince Godric is."

"What have you told Lady Isolda about his disappearance?" I asked.

"I've been telling everyone who asks that the last time I saw him, he was at the docks, talking to a shady-looking sailor."

"Did the family believe that?" I asked. "They must think it odd Prince Godric has vanished."

"Lady Isolda seems unconcerned. Now she has her favorite son back with his betrothed, he's her focus, not the troublesome son who was stirring up a wave of resistance against her."

"What about the sailors?" Griffin asked. "Won't they talk?"

"They won't risk saying a word," Warwick growled out. "They've been told to say nothing. They saw nothing. And they never saw Prince Godric or had anything to do with a cargo of mistreated women."

"You think they'll stick to that story?" Evander asked.

"They've been paid for their silence. And if I hear any of them have broken the agreement, they won't be alive long enough to be full of regrets," Warwick said. "Besides, their ship leaves tonight."

"I didn't take you for a lawbreaker," Evander said to Warwick. "You've gone up in my estimations."

"You remain consistently low in mine."

Evander chuckled and pushed a mug of cherry brandy toward Warwick.

There was another tap on the door, and I discovered Elara and Seraphina. I glanced over my shoulder as my friends chatted and stepped outside. "Have you got the potion for Hodgepodge?"

A tired-looking Seraphina handed over a vial of bright green liquid. "This will reverse the spell, and he'll be back to normal in no time."

"Thanks. I had to leave him in the forest overnight. Neither of us was happy about it. We haven't spent a night apart since we met."

"You'll get him back soon." Elara leaned in close. "The village is alive with talk about Prince Godric vanishing. Would you know anything about that?"

I drew in a breath. Elara and Seraphina had betrayed me and lied to me, and I wasn't ready to take them back into my full confidence. "From what I understand, I doubt he survived the unfortunate situation he found himself in."

Elara's eyes widened. "He's dead?"

"He couldn't have survived what happened to him."

Seraphina sighed. "There's no body to confirm he's dead?"

I shook my head.

"Be careful, Bell," Elara said.

"I'm always careful. It's what's kept me alive this long."

"But things have changed, haven't they?" Seraphina said. "Prince Godric is dangerous and powerful. Keep your wits about you."

I nodded. "Of course. Would you like to come and join us?"

"No, but thank you," Seraphina said. "I have work to do with Emberthorn. Perhaps you'd like to visit him later?"

"Have you gotten him free from the stone?"

"You need to see for yourself. I made progress overnight." A smile flickered across her lips.

"I will. As soon as I've visited Hodgepodge." We nodded our goodbyes, and I closed the door. I returned to my friends and sipped my coffee, tapping my foot on the floor, my thoughts on a hundred different things.

"You look like you need to be somewhere else." Astrid slung an arm around my shoulders.

"Hodgepodge. I've got a potion to reverse the spell that hit him."

"Why would you want to change him? You'll be unstoppable with that enormous beast by your side," Evander said.

"If Hodgepodge wants to stay that size, I'm happy to let him," I said, "but he was getting upset yesterday because he kept bumping into things. And he almost squashed me when he lost his balance."

"Hodgepodge is adorable at any size," Astrid said. "If he wants to go back to being an adorable baby dragon, then let him."

"I need to get to work," Griffin said. "I can walk with you part of the way to the forest."

I nodded, finished my pastry, tidied myself up, then left my friends in my tiny kitchen and headed out with Griffin. The pace was swift, Griffin sensing my desire to be with Hodgepodge.

"That was quite an adventure we went on yesterday," he said.

"I never thought I'd hear myself say this, but despite the risks, I enjoyed it. It felt incredible to help others."

He nodded slowly. "I remember that feeling. When you have value, people notice you."

"You fought bravely. I saw you." I touched his shoulder. "Griffin, you still have value."

"As a general dogsbody."

"You saved lives and protected those women."

"That's kind of you to say, but I have little value other than cleaning up the families' mess. People can't see beyond my appearance."

I let out a sigh. "I know all about cleaning up after the family and learning to be someone I'm not to avoid attention. It's been my whole life."

"Bell!" Gwit hurried over, and I was delighted to see Maggie by his side. "She's back. Can you believe it?"

My gaze met hers, and a flash of understanding passed between us. "That's great news. You must have been on an adventure. I want to hear all about it soon."

She stepped forward and hugged me, her mouth close to my ear. "Thanks, Bell. Don't worry, your secret is safe. None of us will reveal what you did for us."

"I'm so glad she's back," Gwit said. "We have so much catching up to do. And then she's grounded for fifty years."

Maggie stepped back from our embrace and whacked his arm. "You're my dumb brother. You don't get to ground me."

"I do when I'm in charge of the household."

They were laughing as they hurried away, and I continued my walk with Griffin. A few minutes later, one of the other women who'd been on the ship approached me with a small bouquet, which she handed to me. She didn't say a word, simply nodded then walked away.

Tears filled my eyes, and I busied myself with the flowers until my hazy vision cleared.

"You're their hero, Bell," Griffin said. "You helped them when they had no way out. They'll be forever in your debt."

"I don't want anyone feeling they have any debt to repay me," I said.

"You have loyal supporters," he said. "Don't underestimate that. If the Ithric family ever finds out you were involved in Prince Godric's disappearance, they'll come after you. He wasn't the favored prince, but they can't afford to be seen as weak. With allies on your side all over this realm, you have a better chance of survival."

"I'm not just surviving anymore." I lifted the flowers to my nose. "I'm thriving. And so are you. We'll thrive together."

His smile was warm as we reached a fork in the road, and Griffin bid me farewell then headed to work. I continued on into the woods, walking along a barely used path to reach Hodgepodge.

I didn't have to go too far before discovering fresh destruction. Hodgepodge had been stomping around. Shrubs were squashed, branches smashed, and I spotted large footprints in the dirt.

"Hodgepodge," I whispered. "Ready to go home?"

The ground shook as he lumbered into view, swishing his tail. "I'm a clumsy mess. Look at this place. I sneezed earlier and blew over a tree."

I laughed and held up the bottle. "Seraphina found a way to change you. Only if you want to, though."

"I want to! I'm done with being a clumsy-footed, lumbering beastie. And I'm starving. I feel like I need to eat all the time to maintain this size." He sank onto his belly and opened his mouth. "Make me tiny."

I uncorked the vial. "You sure?"

"Positive. Give it to me." He opened his mouth wider. "Make me a wee beastie again who can sit on your shoulder and watch the world go by."

I poured in the potion and stepped back. Hodgepodge shuddered several times, and a swirl of red mist surrounded him. When he came back into view, he was his usual size. I ran over, scooped him up, rested him on my shoulder, and pressed my head against his side.

"It's good to be back where I belong," Hodgepodge said. "Although I'm still starving. I tried hunting last night, but every critter could hear me coming from a mile off and fled. Even a three-legged badger got away."

"Let's get back to the castle. I'll find you something to eat, but then we're visiting the dragons. Seraphina's been hard at work. She said she's made progress."

He snuggled himself around my neck as I strode through the forest, so happy to be reunited with my friend. "Do you trust her?"

"Not completely, but she's making amends," I replied. "And I trust Emberthorn. If he has doubts, then so will I."

When we got closer to the castle, I purchased a stick of dried meat for Hodgepodge from a street stall then had to hide him under my cloak, since my underskirt was still soaked from my adventures at sea.

We slipped inside the castle using the servants' tunnels. Even though it was my day off, people wouldn't think it was strange if they saw me, since my life revolved around the stone dragons. At least, it had until recently.

I checked the time and only had to wait a few minutes until the chamber was empty of visitors. I walked into a poignant silence and absorbed the peace.

"They look the same from this angle," Hodgepodge whispered. "Did Seraphina mess up?"

"Bell!"

I jumped and turned around. Seraphina stood in the entrance to the servants' tunnels, a smile on her face.

"I knew you wouldn't be able to resist a visit. I'm glad you came. Someone is keen to meet you." She led me to Emberthorn.

My gaze ran over him, and I frowned. "He looks the same. It didn't work? The words of release had no effect? Does he need more of my blood?"

"It worked," Emberthorn said as he opened his eyes.

My jaw dropped as his form shimmered, and a glimpse of glossy green scales appeared.

"Seraphina cast a spell over me to ensure the stone illusion remains in place. We don't want to risk terrifying people until they're ready to learn the truth about our return."

"And we don't want the Ithric family knowing what we're doing until Emberthorn is strong enough to get to a safe place," Seraphina murmured. "He's weak after so many years of captivity, and it'll take time to restore him to full strength."

"Stormwing is also gravely ill," Emberthorn said solemnly. "I want him by my side when we approach the family."

"He'll recover?" I looked at Seraphina.

She nodded. "We need time and more magic, but they'll both recover."

I grinned at Emberthorn. "You're really back. I never thought it possible."

"Of course you did. Otherwise, it would never have happened. Your blood, trust, and loyalty ensured our return," Emberthorn said.

I lifted a tentative hand toward his snout, and he nodded. I pressed my palm against him. He was warm, and his scales smooth beneath the illusion magic. "What do we do now?"

"We have a lot to talk about," Emberthorn said. "And as noble and brave as you and your scaled companion are, you won't be able to do this alone."

"Do what alone? Prince Godric is gone. We rescued the women. Life can return to normal."

Seraphina scuffed her feet on the floor. "Emberthorn has plans, and they involve you."

"Oh! I'm open to listening. We should talk about your plans with my friends over cookies and hot cocoa. I didn't do this on my own, so everyone needs to be included."

"Teamwork is the way to go." Emberthorn grumbled a laugh. "And cookies and hot cocoa. I thought you'd never ask. Although if there's a side of roast suckling available, I'd appreciate that, too. My stomach feels like an empty pit."

"Tell me about it! One night as a magical dragon and I'm starved," Hodgepodge said. "I don't know how you do it."

Emberthorn puffed out smoke. "Ah, yes. How did you enjoy being so large?"

"That was you?" I asked.

"I'll always watch over you. I couldn't be with you, so I recruited your excellent scaled companion as a channel for my power. What do you think, Hodgepodge?"

Hodgepodge grunted. "It wasn't terrible. I was able to help Bell when I was that size, so thanks. But how do you deal with the ferocious hunger?"

Emberthorn and Hodgie discussed feasting, while I rested my hands on our newly awakened dragon friend and looked around at the stone chamber in wonderment and all the possibilities it held.

My quiet, cozy life was over, and a new one was beginning. And I'd never been more excited about anything in my life.

Want to find out what's next for Bell and Hodgepodge?
Get Fireside and Stone.

Read on to learn more.

Return to a magical realm full of secrets, strange happenings, and a castle crammed with secrets.

In the quaint otherworldly Ithric realm, a land of magic, castles, and royal households, Bell and her loyal wyvern Hodgepodge, hope that revealing the dragons to the village will be as simple as the perfect recipe for homemade apple pie.

But when statues looking like people who work at the castle show up in alarming numbers, a cozy night in by a warm fire becomes a distant memory. At first, the statues enchant everyone and they're a cute addition to the castle's stone chamber. But then one is destroyed, and Bell discovers there's more to the statues than anyone realizes.

The search for the truth interrupts their haven, and an enemy from Bell's past resurfaces, threatening to destroy everything she loves.

This enchanting blend of cozy mystery and fantasy takes you on a journey with Bell and Hodgepodge as they unravel a tapestry of secrets, face enchanting creatures, and strive to bring light to the shadows that threaten to engulf their beloved home. Will they uncover the secrets in the stone before the world they know is torn apart?

About the Author

K.E. O'Connor (Karen) is the author of the whimsical Fireside mysteries, the adorably fun Lorna Shadow cozy ghost mystery series, the wickedly funny Crypt Witch paranormal mystery series, the Magical Misfits Mysteries featuring a sassy cat with a bundle of twisty puzzles to solve, the slightly darker Witch Haven paranormal mystery series featuring four troubled witches and their wonderful furry (feathered and web-slinging companions), and the delicious Holly Holmes cozy baking mysteries.

Stay in touch with the fun mysteries:

Newsletter: www.subscribepage.com/cozymysteries
Website: www.keoconnor.com
Facebook: www.facebook.com/keoconnorauthor

Printed in Great Britain
by Amazon